When Jerry heard the door slam open, he turned to look at the man who entered.

"What the—" he said

"I told you!" Lori cried. "I told you my husband would be back!"

That was all Clint needed to hear

"Son of a—"

The man's gun belt was hanging on the back of his chair. He went for the gun.

"Don't!" Clint said, but he knew there was no other way. He drew his gun.

"Kill him! Kill him!" the woman shouted, covering her nakedness with her hands and arms.

Clint killed him.

He fired once . . . The impact of the bullet tossed the man onto the table, his arms spread out.

The woman darted forward, grabbed a steak knife from the table, and began stabbing the dead man over and over again . . .

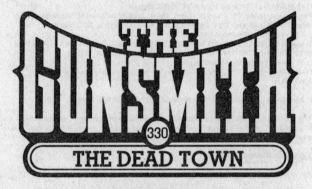

THE GUNSMITH

330

THE DEAD TOWN

J. R. ROBERTS

J

JOVE BOOKS, NEW YORK

THE BERKLEY PUBLISHING GROUP
Published by the Penguin Group
Penguin Group (USA) Inc.
375 Hudson Street, New York, New York 10014, USA
Penguin Group (Canada), 90 Eglinton Avenue East, Suite 700, Toronto, Ontario M4P 2Y3, Canada
(a division of Pearson Penguin Canada Inc.)
Penguin Books Ltd., 80 Strand, London WC2R 0RL, England
Penguin Group Ireland, 25 St. Stephen's Green, Dublin 2, Ireland (a division of Penguin Books Ltd.)
Penguin Group (Australia), 250 Camberwell Road, Camberwell, Victoria 3124, Australia
(a division of Pearson Australia Group Pty. Ltd.)
Penguin Books India Pvt. Ltd., 11 Community Centre, Panchsheel Park, New Delhi—110 017, India
Penguin Group (NZ), 67 Apollo Drive, Rosedale, North Shore 0632, New Zealand
(a division of Pearson New Zealand Ltd.)
Penguin Books (South Africa) (Pty.) Ltd., 24 Sturdee Avenue, Rosebank, Johannesburg 2196,
South Africa

Penguin Books Ltd., Registered Offices: 80 Strand, London WC2R 0RL, England

This is a work of fiction. Names, characters, places, and incidents either are the product of the author's imagination or are used fictitiously, and any resemblance to actual persons, living or dead, business establishments, events, or locales is entirely coincidental.

THE DEAD TOWN

A Jove Book / published by arrangement with the author

PRINTING HISTORY
Jove edition / June 2009

Copyright © 2009 by Robert J. Randisi.
Cover illustration by Sergio Giovine.

ISBN: 978-0-515-14641-7

JOVE®
Jove Books are published by The Berkley Publishing Group,
a division of Penguin Group (USA) Inc.,
375 Hudson Street, New York, New York 10014.
JOVE® is a registered trademark of Penguin Group (USA) Inc.
The "J" design is a trademark of Penguin Group (USA) Inc.

PRINTED IN THE UNITED STATES OF AMERICA

10 9 8 7 6 5 4 3 2 1

ONE

Ghost towns gave the Gunsmith the willies.

The last time he'd ridden into one, he'd been ambushed and almost killed. So, naturally, he didn't like them.

But the dust storm that had come up on him was not leaving him a choice.

He was walking his horse, to keep Eclipse from taking a wrong step in the storm. He had his bandana around his nose and mouth, and could hardly see five feet in front of him. So when the town buildings suddenly appeared, he stopped short and stared.

"Look at that, Eclipse," he said. "A whole town just appeared before us like magic."

Clint started walking again, squinting his eyes against the stinging sand.

The street was empty except for tumbleweed rolling in the wind. Clint had ridden all over southern Kansas over the years, but he did not remember this town.

As he walked Eclipse down the main street, he realized that no one lived here, or had lived here, for many years.

"Looks like we found ourselves a ghost town, boy," Clint said to the Darley Arabian. "Let's see where we can find some shelter from this storm."

As they came abreast of a saloon, Clint decided that was a likely place. The doorway was wide enough to walk Eclipse inside with him.

He walked the horse up onto the boardwalk and through the batwing doors. The relief of being inside was immediate. He pulled the bandana down from his face, used his hands to slap as much sand off of him as he could, then took a look around.

It was a small saloon, with only about half a dozen tables. Of course, that might have been all that was left. There was debris on the floor to indicate there might have been more at one time.

He dropped Eclipse's reins to the floor and walked around. There was enough dust on everything to tell him no one had been there in some time. He went over to the bar, walked around it to check out the bottles that were still in one piece. He found two bottles of whiskey that still had something to offer. He grabbed them and took them to a table, then walked to his horse and got some beef jerky from his saddlebags.

"Sorry, big boy," he said to Eclipse. "I'll see if I can find you some water and something to eat in a little while."

He took the jerky to a table, picked up a fallen chair, and sat down. He munched on the dried meat, washing it down with sips of whiskey. He would have preferred a cold beer, but the whiskey would do in pinch. He knew not to drink too much of it, though. No matter how much of the jerky he ate, his stomach was still going to be pretty empty.

It was getting dark outside. They'd found this town just in time. The wind was still howling, causing the batwings to swing, with some of the sand coming through the door. He got up, walked to the doorway, and tried the regular doors. One was only on one hinge, but he managed to get them to stay closed, quieting the wind and keeping the sand out.

Before the sun went completely down, he carried the jerky and whiskey with him to the back office. There was barely enough light coming through the single window to see a dusty desk and a chair lying on its side, a file cabinet with the drawers open, files in one of them. He'd check that later, if he decided he needed some reading material. It was getting too dark to read anyway, unless he could find a storm lamp. If not, he'd just have to start a fire in the middle of the floor.

He left the office, found an other doorway, and entered a back storeroom. There were two windows in the back wall, but he could hardly see. Luckily, there was a lamp hanging from a post. He grabbed it, shook it, and found enough oil to light it. He didn't know how long it would last, but using the light from that lamp, he found a second one, this one with more oil in it.

He put the last of the jerky in his mouth and balanced the two lamps and the bottle of whiskey as he went back into the saloon.

He put the lighted lamp on the bar and set the other one down on the table he was sitting at. They'd last longer if he lit them one at a time.

By the light of the single lamp he took the saddle off Eclipse. He figured if he couldn't feed him, he might as well make him comfortable. He still had plenty of water in his canteen, so he poured some into his hat and let the horse drink.

In the morning, when the storm had passed, he'd try to find a livery. Maybe there'd be some feed left behind for the big horse.

He drank a little more whiskey, then corked the bottle and put it down. He took one last look around and found a kitchen behind the bar. There was a potbellied stove back there. If it had been colder, he would have broken up a chair, started a fire, and slept in there, but he was comfortable out in the saloon. In the morning, maybe he'd use some of his water to make some coffee, but for now he was satisfied with the jerky and the whiskey warming his stomach.

He was tired from fighting the storm, so he went back into the saloon, made himself comfortable on the floor with his bedroll and saddle, and went to sleep with his gun close by.

TWO

He woke to the smell of bacon.

He rolled over, off his bedroll, grabbed his gun, and stood up. He strapped on the gun and sniffed the air.

"Is that bacon, big boy?" he asked Eclipse. "I thought I was dreaming."

He finished buckling his gun belt and walked to the kitchen. He thought he was going to find someone cooking bacon on the stove, but there was no one there. He walked to the stove and put his hand on it, found it cold.

He lifted his chin and sniffed the air.

Definitely bacon.

There was a door from the kitchen that led outside. He went to it, tried to open it, found it locked. He left the kitchen and went back to the saloon.

"I'm going to go outside and check around," he told Eclipse. "I'll see if I can find something for you to eat, too."

He opened the front doors and walked through the bat-wings into the sunlight.

"Bacon," he said, looking up and down the empty street. "Definitely bacon."

He stepped into the street and walked out to the center.

The calm after the storm was beautiful. Rather than every-thing being covered by sand, it all looked clean and fresh.

There was no one in sight, but the smell of bacon had now been joined by the scent of fresh coffee. Clint picked a direction and started walking.

By the time he found the livery stable, he knew he'd walked the wrong way. The scent of coffee and bacon was gone. Still, he had to find something to feed Eclipse or the horse would be no good to him. He entered the livery and found it empty. Meaning there were no men or horses, and no indi-cation that any had been there for some time. But there was some feed there, enough for Eclipse to have his fill. Rather than try to carry it to the horse, though, he decided to go and get the horse and bring him here.

Walking back to the saloon, he once again picked up the smells of cooking bacon and coffee. His stomach growled, but he decided to get his horse fed first, before he continued to look for wherever and whoever was doing the cooking.

Back in the saloon, he saddled Eclipse so he wouldn't have to carry the saddle himself. Then he took him out of the saloon and walked him to the livery. Once there, he removed the saddle again, poured some of the feed out, and let the horse enjoy it.

"When I get back, I'll get you some water," he said, pat-ting the Arabian's big neck. "Right now I've got to track down that bacon."

He only hoped that whoever was cooking it wouldn't mind sharing.

He reached the saloon and then started walking in the other direction, trying to follow his nose. He was no bloodhound, but he thought the smells were getting stronger.

When he saw the café, he figured that was where it had to be coming from. He stood and watched for a few moments until he saw some white smoke coming from the chimney pipe on the roof.

Okay, this was it. Breakfast. He hoped whoever was cooking wouldn't react badly to his appearance. Maybe whoever it was had also taken refuge from the storm the night before. If they had that in common, maybe it would work in his favor.

He started across the street to the café.

THREE

As he entered the café, he saw that it was pretty much in the same condition as the saloon. Overturned tables and chairs, lots of dust. The only difference was, he saw some footprints in the dust on the floor. Also, in one corner, table and chair had been set upright and cleaned off.

The prints looked like they belonged to a small man, or a woman. The smell of food was stronger than ever, and he headed for the kitchen.

He didn't want to startle anyone, so he called out, "Hello? Anyone here?"

No answer.

The doorway he assumed led to the kitchen had a curtain across it.

"Hello?"

Still no answer.

He approached the curtain, pushed it aside, and entered. As he'd suspected, it was a kitchen—an empty kitchen with a hot stove. He walked to the stove. There was a pot of coffee and a frying pan of bacon. The bacon was hot, but no longer cooking. It had been moved to the back of the stove. From the looks of it, it was nice and crisp. There were three pieces.

He picked up the coffeepot, burned his hand, grabbed a towel, and picked it up again. It was full.

Coffee and bacon.

Since there were only three pieces in the pan, he assumed whoever was cooking had already eaten some.

"Hello?" he called. "Come out. I'm not going to hurt you."

Had whoever it was heard him enter and gone into hiding with the rest of the bacon?

"I'm hungry," he called out. "I'm going to have this bacon and some coffee if you don't come out."

No reply.

He looked around, found no coffee cup. The cook had probably taken a cup.

"I'm going to take this coffee and this bacon over to the saloon with me," he called. "You can find me there."

He was taking a chance, holding the coffee in his left hand and the frying pan in his right. But he didn't have the feeling there was any danger. If there was, he would have to drop the bacon to get to his gun. That would make him mad.

He took the pot and the pan with him, left the café, and walked back to the saloon. He set them both down on the bar, then went to his saddlebag and dug out his coffee cup. He moved around behind the bar and poured himself a cup, then grabbed one piece of bacon and bit off half of it. He chewed thoughtfully and watched the door, washed the bacon down with a sip of coffee.

Maybe whoever had done the cooking would come looking for the coffee.

He was uncomfortable all of a sudden with Eclipse over in the livery, so he decided to go and get him and bring him back. He popped a second piece of bacon into his mouth, had some more coffee, and then left the saloon to go to the livery.

He found Eclipse standing still, having finished feeding. He'd never known the horse to eat too much.

"Had enough, fella?" Clint asked. "Come on, let's go back to the saloon."

He set the saddle on the horse's back, but didn't cinch it in. They walked back up the main street to the saloon. Clint didn't feel as if he was being watched, and that was something he was usually able to feel.

Inside the saloon he took the saddle off Eclipse and set it on the floor. He went back to the bar. The coffeepot was still there, and so was the frying pan.

But the last piece of bacon was missing.

FOUR

He was fairly certain there was only one other person in town with him. What he didn't know was whether or not it was someone else who had taken cover from the storm, or if it was someone who lived there.

Either way, there had to be another horse somewhere. It wasn't in the livery. Maybe it was in one of the other buildings.

He drank some more coffee. There was plenty left, if the other person wanted to come in and have another cup.

He carried the cup outside and stood on the walk in front of the saloon. He looked up and down the street. He hadn't been on his way to anywhere in particular when the storm hit. So he wasn't in any hurry to get anywhere. He could have just mounted up and ridden out, but he was curious about the other person, who had obviously seen him leave the saloon and popped in to grab the last piece of bacon. Could have been watching him right at that moment.

He took a sip of coffee slowly, swallowed it, licked his lips, and went back inside. He hefted the coffeepot. As he suspected, whoever grabbed the bacon had also poured another cup of coffee. He did the same. Whoever it was made good coffee.

He walked around the saloon, again, looking for something, anything, that would give him a clue. When he found nothing, he decided to walk around town, carrying his cup of coffee with him.

He still didn't know what town he had stumbled into. Some of the storefronts still had names on them, but none of them were helpful until he got to the office of the newspaper.

The Jasper Herald.

He was in Jasper, Kansas.

He'd never heard of it.

He tried the front door and found it unlocked. Inside he found newspapers strewn all about the office. He checked a few of them, found them dated five years ago. The stories that he read were boring. Every page he picked up and read had nothing interesting on it.

Jasper, Kansas, had been a boring town.

He left the newspaper office and kept walking until he got to the sheriff's office.

As he walked in, he finished his last sip of coffee. He let the empty cup dangle from the index finger of his left hand. Furniture had been overturned, wanted fliers all over the floor. He checked the cell block. The cell doors were wide open. He walked to the desk, righted the desk chair, and sat down. Opened and closed the drawers, found nothing of interest.

What the hell had happened to this town five years ago?

The gun rack in the sheriff's office was empty.

The shelves in the hardware store and the general store mostly were empty. He did find two cans of peaches in the general store, so he put those in a burlap sack he found and took them with him.

There was a dress shop but no dresses.

A feed store but no feed.

People didn't just up and leave one day; they all moved out. It wasn't a spur-of-the-moment thing.

He went back to the saloon, saddled Eclipse, and walked him out. He continued to walk the town, this time with Eclipse in tow.

Eventually, he came to the doctor's office. It was on the second floor, over an empty store. He went into the store first—empty shelves, broken display cases. From the debris on the floor he thought it might have been an apothecary shop.

He left the shop and walked around to the side of the building, to the stairway. He left Eclipse on his own, untied, and went up the stairs. The door was unlocked, so he walked in.

Two rooms, a waiting room and an examining room. Whoever the doctor was—there was no shingle with a man's name, just one that said "DOCTOR"—he had taken everything with him. Cleaned the place out. However, it still smelled like a doctor's office.

Alcohol.

Sickness.

Death.

There was a desk, but all the drawers were empty. The doctor had moved out. Same time as everyone else? he wondered. Or before?

He heard Eclipse stomping his feet and kicking up a fuss and hurried to the door. When he got outside, the horse was facing out. He had left him facing in. He came down the stairs and stood next to the animal.

"What'd you see, boy?" he asked. "Or hear?"

Eclipse shook his head.

"There's somebody else in this town," Clint said. "Somebody who doesn't want to see us, or be seen."

Ride out, he told himself. What's the difference if it's somebody passing through, or the last person to live here?

Just ride out.

* * *

But he didn't.

He walked farther north, past more run-down shops, an abandoned hotel, some homes that were falling down. He didn't stop walking until he reached the far north end of town, where he stopped dead in his tracks.

When he reached there, he stopped and stared. No homes, no stores, just one structure that had been so well built it was still standing strong.

Leading Eclipse, he walked around the structure, looking at it closely. He thought the ugly thing could have been used today and it would still function.

He finished examining it and walked Eclipse away from it.

"Whatever happened here five years ago," he said to Eclipse, "my bet is that this had a lot to do with it."

He turned and led Eclipse away from what was probably the strongest structure in the whole damned town—a gallows.

FIVE

He walked Eclipse the length of the town, which all in all was only about four or five blocks. There were some outlying buildings to the south, but they were mostly residences that had fallen into disrepair over the years. They didn't look as if anyone had been near them for years. There were no footprints, man or beast.

By the late afternoon he'd pretty much been through all the buildings. He'd found no sign of whoever had cooked the bacon and coffee.

"Come on," Clint said to Eclipse. "We've got to find a place for the night."

It wasn't late, still plenty of daylight, but he wanted to use the daylight to find a place to spend the night—both of them. Come morning, he intended to ride out and forget about who had cooked the bacon and the coffee.

Unless they turned up tonight. Maybe whoever it was would cook dinner, and he could track the cook by the smell. But someone doing that would need the frying pan and coffeepot.

He walked Eclipse back to the saloon and inside. He wasn't surprised to find the pan and the coffeepot gone.

He decided to go upstairs and see if there was a room

with a bed. If not, he'd have to go and find the hotel. There was bound to be one bed still left in town.

Upstairs he found three rooms, all with a bed, so he took the room that overlooked the street. He was still nervous about leaving Eclipse downstairs alone, but he knew the horse would not let anyone come in without kicking up a fuss.

He went back downstairs and closed the front doors, securing them as much as he could. Then he opened one of the cans with his knife, ate the peaches, and shared the water from his canteen with Eclipse. There were no new cooking smells in the air to tease him, so he was satisfied with the peaches.

He decided to rub Eclipse down and give him some of the feed he'd found in the stable. Then he went upstairs to the room he'd picked as his. From the window he stared down at the street. Whoever was in town with him was well hidden, and had also cleverly hidden a horse, or had left.

Unless this person didn't have a horse.

If that was the case, then whoever it was would have to try to steal Eclipse.

Clint sighed. That meant no sleeping in this bed. He turned, grabbed the blanket from the bed and the pillow, and went back downstairs.

"It's you and me, buddy," he said to Eclipse. "Roommates."

He picked a corner, rolled himself up in his bedroll and the blanket, put his head down on the first pillow he'd seen in weeks, and went to sleep.

Gloria Mundy wished she could risk cooking, but the man had already proven he could smell food cooking. Of course, she didn't have to make anything as pungent as bacon or coffee, but that was really all she had left. Supplies in town had finally dried up. After all, she'd been using them for these past three years.

She'd been lucky to stay ahead of the man as he made a search of the entire town. Now he was in the saloon, probably for the night. If she went south of town, to one of the falling-down homes, maybe she could make a fire and heat up the last can of beans without the man smelling it.

Her stomach was growling, so she decided to take the chance.

It was Eclipse who smelled it first.

Clint woke to the horse pounding one hoof on the floor over and over again. He came awake immediately and grabbed his gun.

"What is it, boy?"

He got to his feet. The horse stopped pounding and stood still.

Clint looked around. No one had tried to get in, so it was something else that had bothered the horse. Something he'd not seen but . . . heard? Or smelled?

Smell.

Clint sniffed the air.

"What is that?"

He walked to the front doors and opened them. The night was still, and smells carried on nights like this, especially cooking smells.

He stepped through the batwing doors, stopped, and sniffed the air. Definitely something cooking. Not quite as strong as bacon or coffee, but something . . . and the very distinctive smell of a fire.

People didn't realize that a fire—whether a roaring blaze or simply a campfire—had a very strong, distinctive odor. The ability to smell someone's campfire out on the trail was sometimes the difference between life and death, so it was a smell most traveling men knew well.

SIX

He decided to leave Eclipse where he was and follow his nose again. The big horse could take care of himself. Anyone trying to snatch him was liable to lose a few fingers.

He stepped out into the street, sniffed the air, and picked south. The houses he hadn't bothered going into. It had to be one of those.

The closer he got, the more convinced he was that what he smelled was beans. It had been a long time since beans caused his mouth to water and his stomach to growl. He and Eclipse were also almost out of water. There was a horse trough near the livery, but that water had been there forever. It was filthy, brackish; he wouldn't let Eclipse drink it. If things had become desperate, he would have taken some of that water and boiled it, but things weren't that bad . . . yet.

He reached the end of town and saw it immediately. Someone had taken the chance of building a fire inside one of the houses. He could see the flickering light. Whoever it was must have assumed that he was down for the night.

In getting closer to the house, he passed one of the others. Something drew his eyes. He peered in a window

and saw a horse. It was unsaddled, with a bucket of water
and some feed nearby.

He turned and headed for the other house.

Gloria spooned some of the beans into a plate, grabbed a
fork, sat back, and started eating. She was down to cans of
beans, and that was it. She had enough for a week or so, but
before that she'd be sick of them. She heard a board creak
behind her and instinctively reached for her rifle, which was
leaning against a wall.

"Take it easy," a man's voice said. "I'm not here to hurt
you."

She lowered her head and took a deep breath.

"You smelled the beans?" she asked.

"My horse did," the man said.

"Well," she said, "there's enough here. Help yourself.
There's an extra fork and plate in that burlap bag, over
there."

"Shall we introduce ourselves first?" he asked. "My
name is Clint Adams."

"Gloria," she said.

"No last name?"

"It's never been important."

Clint retrieved the fork and plate, helped himself to
some beans.

"That was your bacon this morning, right?" he asked.

"And my coffee."

"Yes."

"Got any more coffee?"

"I do," she said. "I'll put on a pot, since you're already
here."

He watched her. She had red hair, and the light from the
fire made it appear as if it was ablaze. She was young, in
her twenties, with a big, solid body beneath the man's shirt
and jeans she was wearing.

When the coffeepot was on the fire, she went back to her beans.

"You know," he said, "if you put some bacon in the beans—"

"I used the last of the bacon this morning. The bacon you stole."

"I stole two pieces," he reminded her. "You got the last one."

"Yeah, I did."

"Why were you hiding?" he asked.

"I don't know you," she said.

"Are you afraid of all strangers?"

"I'm careful," she said, "not afraid."

"Did the storm drive you here, like it did me?" he asked.

"No" she said, "I live here."

"Here? In this ghost town? Alone?"

"That's right."

"Did you live here before? I mean, before everyone left?"

"Yes."

"Why didn't you leave, too?"

"This is my home," she said. "Nobody's drivin' me out."

"So the people were driven out?"

"Yes."

"By who?"

"Why are you interested?"

"I've been all over this town," he said. "I've seen the newspaper office, the empty buildings. I've seen the gallows. Why is that still up? Most of the time they're dismantled after the hanging."

"Nobody had time to take it down," she said. "They were all in a hurry to get out."

"Get out? Why?"

"They had to get away before they came."

"Before who came?"

"The gang."

"What gang are we talking about?"

The coffee was ready. She produced another cup, then poured for each of them.

"Thank you," he said, as she handed his to him. "Look, if it helps you, I'll pay for what I eat."

"It doesn't matter."

"Where do your supplies come from? The next town?" he asked.

"They were left over," she said. "I've been living on what was left all this time. It's about gone now, though."

"So you'll have to move on, or go and buy more supplies."

"Maybe," she said. "I don't want to leave here. I might miss—"

She stopped short.

"Miss what?"

She looked across the fire at him.

"Not what," she said. "Who."

"All right," he said, "who might you miss?"

She shook her head.

"It was all because of that hanging."

"Okay, then," he said, "start at the hanging. I'm all ears."

SEVEN

There wasn't a lot to tell.

A woman had been murdered in town, and there was only one stranger around, a man named Pettigrew.

"The whole town decided he did it," she said. "So they had a trial, and built the gallows."

"If they were going to lynch him," Clint asked, "why not just pick out a tree?"

"Oh, no, they said they were gonna do it nice and legal," she said.

"So they found him guilty?"

She nodded. "And they hung him."

"Then what?"

"They buried him in Potter's Field and went on about their business."

"Until?"

"Until a telegram arrived telling the sheriff that the murderer had been caught in El Paso, trying to get into Mexico."

"How did they know he was the killer?"

"He confessed."

"So the town hung an innocent man."

"That's right."

"How did they take it?"

"At first they denied it," she said, "but then the guilt began to seep in. Some folks couldn't take the guilt, so they moved out."

"And the others?"

"The law was still in denial, and so was the mayor. Then another telegram arrived."

"And what did this one say?"

"That Pettigrew had some family, and they were headin' here to take their revenge."

"Family, or was he part of the gang?" Clint asked.

"It was the same thing," she said. "There were a couple of brothers, some cousins, friends of theirs. They all rode in—shooting."

"They kill anyone?"

She nodded.

"Anyone they thought was trying to stand up to them, though not many did. They started with windows and street lamps, finally got around to killing people."

"And then what?"

"They rode out."

"That was it?" Clint asked. "That was their revenge?"

"No," she said, "the leader promised that they were gonna ride in again the following week, and the week after that, and so on."

"And did they?"

She nodded.

"Like clockwork. Shot out windows, killed people, every time they came back. So, finally, people started to leave because no one could stop them."

"The town could have stood together and stopped them," Clint said.

"There wasn't a man with guts among them," she said in disgust.

"What about your father?"

"He was among the first to be killed."

"Why didn't he go to the sheriff, stand with him, maybe?"

She looked across the fire at Clint, who found the sadness in her pretty face heartbreaking.

"My pa *was* the sheriff," she said.

EIGHT

Clint didn't know what to say to that, so he waited until they'd finished their meager meal before speaking again.

"Why didn't you leave, Gloria?"

"I have unfinished business," she said.

"What do you mean?"

"I'm gonna get revenge."

"For the town?"

"To hell with the town," she said. "I'm gonna avenge my father."

"How do you intend to do that?"

"I been practicing with his rifle and handgun," she said.

"How long have you been living here alone?"

She shrugged and said, "About three years."

"And when was the hanging?"

"Four years ago."

"And you've been living here alone all this time?"

She nodded.

No wonder she was leery of strangers. She probably hadn't spoken to anyone for years.

"When was the last time the gang rode into town?" he asked.

"I don't know," she said. "Years."

"And you're still waiting for them to come back?"

"I plan on hunting them," she said. "I got my pa's rifle and handgun. I'm gonna find them."

"When?"

"I was waitin' until I was good enough."

"What have you been eating all this time?"

"I had plenty of food," she said. "All over town. The general store, people's cupboards."

"That has to run out sometime," he said.

"I know," she said. "This was the last of the beans."

"I, uh, took a couple of cans of peaches from the general store. It looked like that was all that was left. I'm sorry. I can return one—"

"That's okay," she said. "A man's gotta eat."

"So when were you planning on starting your hunt?" he asked.

"A day or so," she said. "I got my horse hid in one of the other houses."

He didn't bother telling her that he'd seen it.

"Gloria . . . how many times has the gang been back since everybody left?"

"A lot," she said. "They came back every week for six months after the last person left."

"I wonder why they didn't burn it down," he said. "Or knock down that gallows."

She shrugged.

"Gloria, if you know who those men are, you should go to the law."

"They killed the law."

"Go to St. Joe, to the federal authorities, and tell them what you know."

"It won't make a difference," she said. "I'll hunt them myself."

"How old are you?"

"Twenty-two."

"You've never killed a man before. What makes you think you can?"

"I can," she said. "The hate that burns inside me says I can."

He got up, stared down at her.

"I'm leaving in the morning," he said. "You're welcome to ride along for a while, if you like."

"That's okay," she said. "I'm used to bein' alone."

"Suit yourself," he said, "but I'll be leaving from the saloon at first light, if you change your mind."

"I won't."

"Thanks for the beans," he said. "Sorry they were your last."

"Had to run out, sometime."

He stared down at her, realized that with a scrub and a nice dress she'd look real pretty. It was a shame that hate was going to eat that up eventually.

He slept fitfully in the saloon, then got up early and saddled Eclipse. He looked over at the lone can of peaches sitting on the bare floor, thought about leaving them, but eventually shoved them into his saddlebag.

Briefly, he thought about forcing his help on Gloria, but in the end he decided that wasn't a good idea. When he walked out of the saloon to mount Eclipse, he found her waiting out there for him, on foot.

"I need help," she said.

"Well," he said, "I guess I don't have to leave today."

NINE

He stayed another week. Gloria had a stash of food that lasted just about that long. He worked her with a rifle, and then with a handgun. The pistol she had was an old Colt that belonged to her father. At first Clint thought she should replace that gun as soon as possible, but he found that she had a natural aptitude with it. She was fairly adept with the rifle, but after only two days she began to excel with the handgun. All he had to do was get her to "squeeze" the trigger rather than "pull," and "point" the gun rather than "aim" it.

Clint continued to sleep in the saloon while Gloria remained at the house. They did their shooting behind the house, and also had their meals there.

On the last night, they finished off the remnants of the food.

"I'm going to ride west tomorrow," he said, "heading for Colorado. You're welcome to come along."

"I think I'm going to go east, into Missouri," she said. "I have a friend in Joplin who might be able to give me some information."

"Well, suit yourself," he said. "My offer stands if you want to meet me in front of the saloon in the morning."

"Thank you."

They drank coffee in silence, each alone with private thoughts.

"Clint?"

"Yes."

"Do you think I'm ready?"

"You have a natural aptitude with a handgun, Gloria," he said, "but are you ready to take on a gang of outlaws? No. It's more than likely you'll end up getting killed."

"That's what I thought you'd say."

"But you're still going to go after them?"

"Yes," she said. "I don't have a choice."

"I can actually understand that," he said.

Gloria cleared away the debris of their meal and stoked the fire that she'd also be sleeping next to. She pulled out her bedroll and blanket as Clint stood, preparing to leave.

"You've been real generous, Clint," she said, turning to face him. "Can I ask one more favor?"

"Sure," Clint said. "If I can do it, it's yours."

"Would you stay here with me tonight?" she asked.

"Gloria—"

"I ain't never been with a man."

"You're a virgin?"

"Well, no," she said, "I mean, I been with boys, I just ain't never been with a man. If I'm gonna die soon, I'd like to know what it's like, just once . . . at least."

In the flickering firelight she was very beautiful. He was suddenly sad that she might be going to her death, but this was something she had to do, and he knew she had to do it alone. There was no way he could go with her, commit a good part of his life to her quest, but he could at least do this for her.

He moved closer to her, took her by the shoulders, and kissed her. She moaned into his mouth and leaned into him. He unbuttoned her shirt and slid his hand inside to cup one of her firm, young breasts. He flicked the nipple with his thumb as he kissed her neck, and she sighed.

He pulled her shirt free from her belt so he could completely unbutton it and remove it. Her skin glowed in the light from the fire. Her breasts were like large, ripe peaches, fitting nicely in his hand, her pink nipples stiff beneath his thumbs.

Returning the favor, Gloria unbuttoned Clint's shirt and pulled it off him, started kissing his neck and shoulders. Briefly they parted long enough to remove their gun belts, boots, and trousers, and then, naked, they came back together. As he pulled her to him, running his hands over her back and buttocks, her skin burned him. He kissed her shoulders, her breasts, tongued her nipples until she groaned and went weak-kneed. He eased her down onto her back on the blanket, determined to give her a night she could remember. Maybe it would even be such a pleasurable night that she would decide to go on living rather than try to hunt the Pettigrews down.

He continued to roam her body with his mouth and his hands. He kissed her breasts while sliding his hand down between her legs. She stiffened for just a moment when he touched her, but then relaxed and let her legs fall open. When she was very wet, he removed his hand, and kissed his way down over her belly until he was settled between her legs. He kissed the soft skin of her thighs, breathed in the scent of her excitement, and then finally pressed his tongue and mouth into the damp tangle of pubic hair. She jerked at the moment he touched her, but then sighed and relaxed, reaching down to cup his head and hold him there. He licked and kissed her, enjoying not only the scent but the taste of her. Eventually he slid his hands beneath her buttocks and lifted her up, held her there so he had easier access to her. At that point her belly began to tremble. She closed her hands into fists, wrapping her fingers in his hair, and then, at the moment her excitement overtook her, she lifted her hips and pressed herself even more tightly to his face as his tongue entered her . . .

Not much later, when Gloria had regained her breath, she took Clint's rigid penis in her hand and slid down between his legs to explore him with a murmured "My turn . . ."

She pressed him to her face, licking the length of him until he was very wet, and then taking him into her mouth. She suckled him while closing her fist around the base of him and using her other hand to lightly caress his testicles.

When Clint thought he could stand no more, he reached down for her and forcefully pulled her up on top of him. She grabbed his hard cock, pressed it to her soaking vagina, and sat down on him so that he was deep inside of her. She began to rock on him then, while he pawed her firm breasts, the flickering firelight throwing shadows on her. Finally, she lay down flat on him, bouncing her buttocks up and down with more and more speed until they both cried out in a mixture of pleasure and exquisite pain . . .

TEN

TWO MONTHS LATER . . .

Clint saw the light.

No, he didn't see God. He actually saw a light in the distance. That was a good sign. It was snowing, and his jacket wasn't exactly keeping the cold off him. Why he had ever thought to go to Minnesota in February was beyond him.

He patted Eclipse's broad neck and said, "We're going to head for that light, boy, and hope it's coming from a fire."

Eclipse didn't mind the cold, but Clint didn't have the same kind of coat the Darley Arabian did.

"Let's move, big boy," Clint said. "Maybe there's hot coffee there as well."

Lori Gregory put a plate of food on the table in front of the man who's foul body odor permeated the entire house.

"Get me some more coffee!" he barked.

"Right away."

The man had kept her in the house for five days now, since he first arrived and asked if she could part with an extra blanket. Instead of taking the blanket and leaving, he'd forced his way into the house and taken her prisoner.

She tried to tell him that her husband would be coming back home soon, but the man didn't believe her. Or he didn't care. If her husband hadn't already died the year before, he would certainly have been in danger now.

She didn't know what to do. She was just waiting for an opportunity to get away, but the man was very careful not to give her any openings. He tied their legs together, her left to his right, when they went to bed at night—after he was finished raping her. If she couldn't find a way to escape soon, she thought suicide might end up being her only answer.

She poured him some more coffee, and thought briefly about throwing the hot liquid into his face.

"Don't even think about it, girl," he told her, as if reading her mind. "Even if you blinded me, I'd grab you and snap your neck."

His name was Jerry, and she was totally cowed by him. She believed every threat he made.

"All right."

He sipped the coffee, made a face, then sipped it again. She waited to see if *he* would throw it at *her*. When he didn't, she heaved a small sigh of relief and went back to the stove.

"Bring me some more potatoes."

She looked in the pot. There were more potatoes, but not a lot more. She hoped these would be enough to satisfy him.

"Come on," Jerry shouted. "I need more food. I got to keep up my strength. You think it's easy rapin' you every night?"

She closed her eyes, fighting back tears. If it was only once a night that he raped her, she might have been able to handle it.

Clint rode to within sight of the small house. The light was shining from the windows. Next to the house was a small barn. He decided to get a closer look on foot, rather than just ride on up.

He dismounted and dropped Eclipse's reins to the ground. Snow crunched beneath his boots, but he was sure it couldn't be heard inside. As he neared the barn, he suddenly heard a man's voice shouting from inside the house. He couldn't make out what was being said, but somebody was mad.

There were two horses in the barn, only one of which was used to pull a plow or a buggy. The other looked like a decent trail horse that had been ridden a long way—and ridden hard.

More shouting from the house. He left the barn and moved closer to the main structure. From the outside it looked like a two-room house. A husband and wife, maybe one child.

He got to one window and peered in. A man was seated at a table, a woman standing next to him. He had hold of her wrist and he wasn't treating her gently. But if he was her husband, she was used to it.

Clint decided to just watch, and wait.

"This is all that's left?" he asked.

"I'm sorry," she said, "I didn't—"

"You ate too much!" he said, grabbing her wrist. "Bitch!"

He stood up and slapped her, then reached out, grabbed the front of her dress, and pulled. He tore the garment from her so that she was completely naked. He forbade her to wear underwear.

He reached out and grabbed a breast that was already bruised.

"I'll teach you to eat my supper," he said.

Clint watched only until the man tore the dress from her body. Husband or not, that was no way to treat a woman.

He ran to the front door, lifted his right foot, and lashed out.

When Jerry heard the door slam open, he turned to look at the man who entered.

"What the—" he said.

"I told you!" Lori said. "I told you my husband would be back!"

That was all Clint needed to hear.

"Son of a—"

The man's gun belt was hanging on the back of his chair. He went for the gun.

"Don't!" Clint said, but he knew there was no other way. He drew his gun.

"Kill him! Kill him!" the woman shouted, covering herself up with her hands and arms.

Clint killed him.

He fired once. The man never got his gun clear. The impact of the bullet tossed him onto the table, his arms spread out.

The woman darted forward, grabbed a steak knife from the table, and began stabbing the dead man over and over again.

Clint's first instinct was to stop her, but he knew she had probably suffered a lot at the hands of this man, so he let her continue until finally she slumped to the floor, exhausted.

ELEVEN

Clint took the body outside and left it in the snow. He didn't know what he was going to do with it come morning. When he came back into the house, the woman had a robe wrapped around her and was hugging herself as if it was cold, despite the fact that the oven and the fireplace were keeping the house fairly warm.

"My name is Clint Adams," he said. "I wish I could have introduced myself before the shooting started. What's your name?"

"Are you like him?" she asked.

"I don't understand," he said. "Am I like—what was he like?"

"Do you plan to stay around for a few days, rape me two or three times a day?"

"Ma'am," Clint said, "I just rode up to your house because I saw the light. When I looked in the window and saw what was happening, I thought you needed help. If you like, I'll leave—"

"No," she said, "no . . . I don't want to be alone."

"What's your name?"

"Lori Gregory."

"I'm sorry for what that man did to you, Lori," he said. "How long . . . I mean . . ."

"He's been here five days," she said. "He's beaten me, and raped me, and made him serve me for five days."

"But . . . your husband . . ."

"He's dead," she said. "He died last winter."

"But you told that man—"

"I told him my husband was comin' back, but he didn't believe me. But he said if I was tellin' the truth, he'd kill my husband when he came back."

Quick thinking on her part, he thought. Make the man think that Clint was the husband so he'd go for his gun.

"I'm sorry," she said. "It was all I could think of . . ."

"You could use a doctor, Lori," he said. "What's the nearest town? I'll take you—"

"Can we do that in the morning?" she asked. "You look tired, and I haven't slept in five nights."

"He didn't let you sleep?"

"He tied our legs together so I couldn't slip out of bed. I couldn't sleep that way."

"No, I don't suppose you could."

"If you don't mind, Mr. Adams, I'm going to try to get some sleep. The stove is still hot, if you want to fix yourself somethin' to eat."

"I'm obliged, Lori."

"No," she said, "I'm the one who's obliged. I think he might have killed me this time."

"What set him off?"

"I guess I didn't make enough potatoes."

"Well . . . go and get some sleep. I'm going to see to my horse, and then I'll come back in and make use of your stove. After that, I'll bed down in the barn—"

"No," she said, "you'll freeze to death."

"I don't want you to be uncomfortable, thinking I might—"

"It's okay," she said. "I don't think you're like him."

"Thanks."

"But if you are," she said, "I'll have a knife in the bedroom with me. If you do try to come in, I'll use it . . . on myself. I probably should have killed myself days ago, but I think I was too much of a coward then."

"Lori—"

"Have a good meal, and a good night, Mr. Adams," she said. "We can talk again in the morning."

She headed for the bedroom.

"Just one more question?"

She stopped in the doorway. "Sure."

"Did you know his name?"

"Yes," she said. "He said his name was Jerry Pettigrew."

TWELVE

Clint was able to make himself a steak before turning in. He undid his bedroll by the fireplace and removed only his boots.

Lying on his back, staring at the ceiling, he wondered about the man named Pettigrew he'd been forced to kill. He hadn't heard the name since he was in the ghost town of Jasper, Kansas, and he had heard it from Gloria—a young woman whose last name he had never learned.

Coincidences. He hated them. There had to be a lot of men named Pettigrew. It didn't mean that this one was from the same family of killers.

He turned his back to the fire. Abusive though the man was, he felt badly about leaving him lying out in the snow. Some hungry critters were bound to get to him before Clint could bury him—if he could bury him in the frozen ground. He'd probably be better off taking him into the next town and dropping him off at the undertaker's. Of course, he'd have to do some explaining to the local sheriff first.

Clint woke some time later, drew his gun from his holster, then quickly turned. It was Lori. She had crept into the room, holding her robe closed with both hands. The room was well lit by the fire, and he could see that her hands were empty. He holstered his gun and got to his feet.

"Are you all right, Lori?"

"Thomas," she said, "come to bed. It's late."

"Thomas?"

She must have thought he was her dead husband. Maybe she was sleepwalking. Or just in shock.

"Lori," he said, approaching her cautiously, "I'm not Thomas. I'm Clint. Remember?"

She was looking at him, but her eyes weren't focused.

"Tommy," she said, suddenly becoming coquettish. "Come to bed, Tommy. Keep me warm."

She moved her hands and the robe fell open. Her breasts were peach-sized, and he could see the bruises on them. He thought the best thing he could do for her was get her back into bed.

"Okay, Lori," he said, "let's go to bed."

He took her by the arm, turned her toward the bedroom door, and moved her that way, using just the slightest bit of pressure. She went along willingly, right up to the bed.

Clint got her to lie down, but she put her arms around his neck and wouldn't let go.

"Lie down with me, Tommy," she pleaded, "make love to me. Make it all go away."

She held onto him tight, as if for dear life. He decided to help her get to sleep. He'd just lie down with her and hold her until she fell asleep.

"All right, Lori," he said. "Scoot over."

She moved over and let him get into bed with her. She snuggled against him, her robe wide open. He tried to close it, but it had gotten pinned under her and bunched. She might as well have been naked.

"Thomas," she said, pressing her face into the crook of his neck, "you came home."

"It's all right, Lori," Clint told her. "Go to sleep."

But sleep was not what this young woman had in mind.

That was obvious from the way she started running her hands over Clint's body. She started to unbutton his shirt, undo his jeans; she tried to put her hand down the front of his pants. He struggled with her a bit, but he really couldn't move in any way that didn't bring her bare flesh into play. Her skin was smooth, and very hot, and Clint was only human. He felt his body reacting to her nearness, her touch, her scent.

"Lori, no—"

"Please," she said, "don't make me beg. I need you to . . . clean me."

Clint felt bad for her, but he also knew he'd feel bad if he had sex with her. She was in shock and was not herself.

"Lori, I . . . I can't."

He slid from her grasp and from her bed, went back to the other room and his bedroll. He could hear her crying in her bedroom, but he turned a deaf ear to it—or tried to— and lay back down.

He turned his back to the fire and closed his eyes. Before long the crying stopped and he was able to drift off to sleep . . .

He was having a dream, and it was waking him up. He dreamt there was a woman down between his legs, using her mouth on him. When he looked down he saw the top of her head as she bobbed up and down. Then, fairly quickly, he realized it wasn't a dream, and the one sucking him was Lori. Somehow, she'd gotten his pants off while he was asleep. If she'd been a man with a gun, he would have been dead. That made him angry, at himself.

"Lori—" he said, reaching for her.

She released him from her mouth and smiled lasciviously.

"Just enjoy it, Thomas," she said.

"I'm not—" he started, but she cut him off by straddling him and quickly taking him inside her wet, steamy depths.

"Oh God," she said, riding him up and down. He was full awake now, and way past the point of resisting.

"All right, damn it," he growled.

He grabbed her, turned her over, and started to fuck her hard.

"This is what you wanted, right, Lori?"

"Yes, Thomas," she said, "yes. Oh, yes, clean me, please clean me . . ."

If she thought sex with her husband was going to cleanse her from the days she had spent with Pettigrew, who was he to dissuade her?

She wrapped her legs around him. She glowed as the light from the fire bathed her. She smiled, then she laughed, urging him on in every way she could—talking, touching, clutching him to her, rising up to meet the thrust of his hips with her own.

Why should he feel bad about giving her what she wanted?

THIRTEEN

Clint walked Lori back to her bed, and this time the woman stayed there with no complaining or crying. In fact, he could hear her rhythmic breathing before he got back to his bedroll.

In the morning he woke when she came out of her room, but he remained still and watched her awhile. She puttered around the kitchen and seemed about to begin cooking breakfast.

The big question was, when she saw him, would she still think he was her husband, Thomas? Or would she remember it was him? Or would she have forgotten the whole thing completely?

He rolled over, deliberately making noise.

"Good, you're awake," she said. "Would you like some breakfast?"

"That would be nice," he said, getting to his feet.

"There's a bucket of water over there," she said. "You can use it to wash up."

"Thanks."

He washed his hands, arms, and face, still wondering if she thought he was Thomas or himself.

He dried off, turned, and walked to the table.

"I can make some flapjacks," she said.

"Great."

"And coffee."

She came over with a cup and set it down in front of him. He looked up at her, but she never met his eyes.

"Lori—"

"Are you going to bury that man?" she asked. "Petti-grew?"

Okay, she remembered last night, and knew he wasn't Thomas. But did she remember anything else?

"The ground's too hard. I think I'll just throw him over his saddle and take him to town."

"And what will you tell the sheriff?"

"The truth."

"Will I . . . have to come with you?"

"No," Clint said, "I think I'll be able to get the sheriff to come out here and listen to your story."

"That's good."

He was starting to smell the flapjacks. Before long he had a stack of them in front of him. She sat across from him with a cup of coffee.

"You're not eating?"

"I'm not hungry," she said. "I haven't been hungry for days."

He couldn't blame her for that.

"Your appetite will come back," he told her.

"I hope so," she said. "You haven't told me what brought you here."

"Well, I saw your lights and they looked so warm—" he started.

"No, I mean to Minnesota."

"Oh," he said. "Actually, I'm not going anywhere in particular. Just passing through."

"Why would you want to pass through here, in this weather?" she asked, shivering.

"I'm asking myself the same question," he said. "Lori,

maybe you should come to town with me and see the doctor."

"When my husband was alive, I did all the mending," she said. "It didn't matter what it was—a shirt, a dress, or a broken bone. I don't have any broken bones, Clint, just some bruises."

"Yes, but—"

"And once you talk to the sheriff, everyone in town will know what happened. I . . . I don't want them all looking at me."

"You'll have to go to town sometime."

"I know," she said, "just not right now."

"It's your choice."

She watched him while he ate, then sat back in her chair.

"I'm sorry," she said. "I used to watch my husband eat."

"It's okay," he said. "I don't mind."

She poured him a second cut of coffee.

"When you introduced yourself last night, I didn't real-ize . . . who you really were. I remembered when I woke up this morning."

"I see."

"I'm really in debt to you."

"You would be no matter who I am," he said.

"I . . . I know," she said. "I just . . . appreciate what you did. Another man would have just kept going."

"A lot of men, but not all."

"Most."

She was probably right. Most men, looking in the win-dow and seeing what was going on, would have moved on, or would have knocked instead of kicking the door in.

"I'll see about getting the body on the horse," he said. "I'll let you know before I leave."

"Will you . . . I mean, are you gonna come back?"

"I don't know," he said. "My plan was just drift for a while, but the snow and the cold are making me second-guess myself."

"But . . . if the sheriff comes back to question me . . . ," she said.

"But what, Lori?"

"I'll be . . . alone with him."

"Do you know the sheriff?"

"No," she said. "My husband knew him, though. He used to go into town all the time. I . . . hardly ever went in at all."

He thought a moment, then said, "All right, if he wants to come out here right away, I'll come along with him."

"That would make me feel better," she said. "Thank you."

"Thanks for breakfast," he said, standing up. "I better see to the body, and the horses."

He stood there a moment. She stared up at him, but said nothing. He couldn't read anything in her eyes. She seemed to have no knowledge of what had transpired last night.

He thought that was good—very good.

FOURTEEN

Joe Pettigrew smacked the ass of the girl who was crouched on her hands and knees in front of him. He smacked it again, left cheek, so that it glowed rosy red like the right cheek did.

"Come on, baby," she said, wiggling her big butt at him.

"Shut up, whore!" he snapped.

"I just want you so bad—"

He slapped her ass, harder this time.

"Hey!" she cried. "That hurt."

"Then shut the hell up!"

He stroked his penis a few times, then drove it between her thighs and into her as hard as he could. She cried out once, but as soon as he started fucking, she got into the rhythm with him. She drove her ass back into him so he could go as deep as possible.

"There, bitch!" he growled each time her flesh slapped his. "How's that, bitch!"

"Is that all you got?" she asked, making him mad.

"Oh, you gotta learn, bitch," he said. "When I'm finished fucking you, you gotta learn."

And she would . . .

* * *

"Where's Joe?" Lyle Pettigrew asked.

"I think he's with that whore," their cousin, the one they called Nutty, said.

"And where's your brother?"

The fourth Pettigrew was Deacon.

"I think he's asleep."

"Still in bed?"

"What do we got to do while we're waitin' on Jerry?" Nutty Pettigrew asked. "Sleep, or go find a whore. Either one means you're in bed."

Lyle and Nutty were sitting in the saloon, nursing beers while they waited for Jerry, who was five days late, to arrive.

"What the hell is holdin' Jerry up?" Nutty asked.

"I don't know," Lyle said. He had more patience than his brothers and cousins, but even he was starting to wonder. "At least there's no law lookin' for us in this state," he said.

Lyle thought all the other Pettigrews were stupid and, without him, would all probably be in jail. "He better not damage that whore," he said, referring to his brother Joe.

"What's the difference?" Nutty said. "There's no sheriff in this mud puddle."

Lyle dry-washed his face with both hands.

"And we don't need to be, Nutty," he said. "Understand?"

"Lyle," Nutty admitted, "I only ever understand half of what you say."

Nutty Pettigrew was the enforcer of the gang. He was quick with his fists, faster still with a gun. Lyle's brain tried to keep his family out of trouble, and when they finally found it, it was Nutty who got them out—following Lyle's directions.

"Maybe I'll use the whore after Joe's finished," Nutty said.

"Never mind," Lyle said. "You don't need no whore. Besides, by the time Joe's done with her she probably won't be good to nobody for a while."

"Why does he like to do that?"

"Hurt women?"

Nutty nodded.

"Because he likes it," Lyle said. "In fact, he likes it just a little too much."

FIFTEEN

The nearest town was Bedford.

Clint got the now frozen body of Jerry Pettigrew draped over his horse, then saddled Eclipse. He went back to the house to tell Lori he was ready to go.

"Are you sure you won't change your mind?"

"No," she said, hugging herself. "I'll wait here."

"Okay," he said. "Do you have a gun in the house?"

"Yes, my husband's rifle."

"Well, carry it with you when you answer the door from now on."

"That was my plan."

"All right, then. You said the next town is Bedford, right?"

"That's where my husband used to go for supplies."

"Stay here and wait, Lori, okay?" Clint said. "Don't go anywhere."

"I've got nowhere to go, Clint," she told him. "No friends."

He was tempted to force her to come with him, but in the end he mounted up and left, leading Pettigrew's horse.

Bedford turned out to be a small town, just a stop in the road for a drink and supplies. It was late afternoon when

Clint arrived. They'd had to move slowly in the snow, mainly moving at the body-laden horse's pace.

He rode the length of the street and did not see a sheriff's office. He did, however, spot the undertaker's, so he went there. He reined Eclipse in, tied off the dead man's horse, and stepped up to the front door. Written on the glass of the door was the name "WALTER DEADLY."

He stepped inside and stomped his feet to get snow off his boots.

"May I help you, sir?"

He turned and saw a man of medium height, wearing a suit a banker would be proud of.

"Are you the undertaker?

"That's me."

"Walter Deadly?" Clint asked.

"That is my name."

"That's kind of . . ."

"Odd?" the man asked. "Yes, many people comment on it."

"So is that why you became an undertaker?" Clint asked. "Because of your name?"

The man frowned and said, "I don't follow."

"Never mind. I have a dead man outside."

"How did the poor deceased fellow die?" the man asked.

"I shot him."

"Oh, dear."

"It was self-defense. I notice you don't have a sheriff in town?"

"We do, kind of," Deadly said.

"But I didn't see any office."

"Yes, well, we haven't gotten around to building one yet.

"So where's the sheriff hang his hat?"

The undertaker waved his hands and said, "Right here."

"You share the office with him?"

"In a manner of speaking." The man pushed back his jacket, revealing a tin star pinned to his vest.

"I share the office, and the job."

"Huh," Clint said, "I've never run into anyone who held both those jobs before."

"First time for everything," Deadly said. "So tell me again how you came to shoot this man."

SIXTEEN

"Since you're the sheriff," Clint said, after telling Deadly his story, "I expect you'll want to ride out and question . . . Lori."

"I'm sure Mrs. Gregory will back up your story, Mr. Adams," Walter Deadly said.

"So you're not going to go out?"

"I don't think I need to. Besides, I'm more like the honorary sheriff, you know? Until they can find somebody permanent."

"So you're really the undertaker."

"That is my calling, yes sir. I can take the body from you and prepare it for burial. Would you like to pick out a casket?"

"No," Clint said, "since I killed him, I guess I might as well pay to have him buried, but that doesn't mean I'm going to spend a lot of money. Just . . . wrap him in something."

"Very well," Deadly said. "That will be two dollars, please."

"Is that the cheapest you've got?"

"The two-dollar burial is the cheapest, yes."

Clint took the money out and handed it over.

"Come on," he said. "The body's a little stiff. I'll help you bring it in."

"I'd be much obliged," Deadly replied.

"Obliged enough to take a dollar off the burial?"

"Not that obliged," Deadly said.

"I was just kidd— Oh, never mind."

Clint was at a loss about what to do. If Sheriff Deadly—willingly or not, he was the law—wasn't going to ride out to talk to Lori Gregory, then how would she know that everything was all right?

There was no choice really. He was going to have to ride back to her house to let her know. He'd have to head out in the morning, as it was getting too cold now and would be dark before he got there.

"Where can I get a good meal?" he asked the undertaker, after they had moved the body inside.

"There's a café down the street called Maisy's," Deadly said. "Makes a good steak."

"Thanks."

"Hey," Deadly said as Clint was walking out. "He got any kin?"

"A lot," Clint said. "I don't think you want them coming here, though."

Clint went to Maisy's for that steak and found it pretty good. The coffee was also hot and black, the way he liked it. And the woman serving him—who may or may not have been Maisy—did her job quietly. Clint figured she wasn't in the habit of talking to her customers, since she probably didn't get much practice.

When he'd finished eating and paid his bill, he asked her, "This town got a saloon?"

"We got one," she said. "Across the street. Got a sign out front used to say 'Blackjack Saloon.' Pretty faded now."

"Thanks."

She was right about the sign. All he could make out was "Bl-j--k Sal--n."

He went inside and found the place empty except for the bartender and two men sitting at a table.

"Help ya?" the bartender asked.

"A beer."

"Comin' up."

When it came, Clint was surprised to find it so cold, then realized that any time he'd ever had a beer in Minnesota—no matter how big or small the saloon—it was always cold. Given the weather, why was that so hard to believe?

"Thanks," Clint said. "Anything to do in this town?"

The man shrugged. "We got a whore."

"That's okay," Clint said. "No poker games?"

"Not around here," the man said. "Folks here like to hold onto their money."

"What about these two fellows?" Clint asked.

"For poker?" Again, he shrugged. "They're strangers, like you. Been here a few days, but still strangers. You'll have to ask them."

"Maybe I will."

Clint eyed the two men, using the mirror behind the bar to do it. They didn't seem to be paying any mind to him at all. He found that odd, not because of who he was, but because it's just human nature to be curious.

Unless the two men just didn't want to be paid any attention themselves.

SEVENTEEN

Clint decided to leave the two men to themselves. He called the bartender and waved for another beer.

"Is there a hotel in town?" he asked, as the man put down the beer.

"No," the bartender said, "but we got some rooms upstairs."

"Anything available?"

"We got a couple."

"How much?"

"Two dollars a day."

"Two dollars?"

"Did I say there's no hotel in town?" the man asked grimly.

"Good point," Clint said. "Okay." He dug out two dollars and gave them to the man.

The bartender accepted the money and handed over a key.

"Room five."

"The two gents behind me," Clint asked, "do they have rooms?"

"One room for the two of them," the barkeep said, leaning in and keeping his voice as low as Clint's. "They're in room three."

"Thanks. Where can I bed down my horse?"

"Got us a small stable out back, if you want. Used to be a livery in town, but it's empty now. You could put him there for free, if you want, but you won't find no feed there."

"Uh-huh," Clint said. "How much for out back?"

"Four bits."

Clint dropped the coins on the bar.

"Obliged," the bartender said.

Clint pocketed his key. He'd bed down Eclipse and then take his gear to his room.

"Any other strangers in town besides these two?" he asked.

"Might be," the bartender said, "but if there are, they ain't come in here."

Clint nodded and the bartender left him to his second beer.

"You know that fella?" one of the men sitting at the table asked the other.

"Never seen him before," the second man said.

"Well, I have," the first man said. "That's Clint Adams."

"The Gunsmith?"

"That's right."

"Oh, man . . ." The second man leaned forward in his chair.

"You wanna try him?"

"We ain't gettin' nothin' else done in this one-horse town."

"We take Adams here," the first man said, "and we'll put this one-horse town on the map, like Hickok did Deadwood."

The second man licked his lips. "You wanna do it now?"

The first man nodded. "As soon as he heads for the door."

"In the back?" the second man asked.

"You know a better way?"

"Uh, n-no," the second man said. He was suddenly nervous, but didn't want his partner to know.

"Okay then," the first man said. "Wait for my move."

Clint finished his beer.

"I'm going to see to my horse, and then check out my room," he called out to the bartender.

"Suit yourself."

Clint turned and headed for the batwing doors.

"Now!" the first man hissed at his partner.

The second man was so nervous, so anxious, that he started to ride to his feet to draw his gun, and slid his chair back.

Clint heard the chair slide on the floor, turned, and drew. He dropped into a crouch and fired quickly four times. The two men danced in place a bit as the lead hit them, and then fell over, one draped over the table, the other on the floor.

"J-Jesus!" the bartender yelled.

"You better go and get your undertaker–sheriff, Bartender," Clint said, ejecting the spent shells from his gun.

"Y-yessir."

"I'll wait here."

EIGHTEEN

Walter Deadly came into the saloon, looking every inch the undertaker—except now he was wearing a gun on his hip.

"Bartender said there's been some excitement," Deadly said to Clint, who was lounging on the bar with another beer.

"Those two tried to back-shoot me," Clint said. "I hate back-shooters."

Deadly walked to the two men and checked them to be sure they were dead.

"Any idea why?" he asked.

"Well, either they were trying to make a name for themselves," Clint said, "or they were looking to rob me . . ."

"Or?"

Clint shrugged. "Revenge? Maybe they were waiting for the man I brought in."

Deadly looked at the bartender.

"Jeff, they say anythin' about waitin' here for somebody?"

"Not a word, Sheriff."

Deadly leaned over and went through the pockets of both men. He found a letter in one of their pockets.

"Ever hear of a Leonard David?" he asked Clint.

"No," Clint said. "So his name's not Pettigrew?"

"I guess not," Deadly said, "or maybe he's just carryin' this David's mail."

"Nothing in the other one's pocket?"

"No," Deadly said, "but I did find twenty dollars."

"That ought to pay for their burials," Clint said.

"Jeff, you back his story?" Deadly asked.

"You bet, Walter," the bartender said. "As soon as he headed out the door, they stood up and drew their guns. They was gonna shoot him in the back, all right."

"Okay then," Deadly said. "I'll get somebody to move these bodies. You stayin' the night?"

"I've got a room upstairs."

"One night?"

"Just one night."

"Good."

Clint put the empty mug down on the bar.

"Now, like I said before, I'm going to see to my horse and then go to my room."

In the nearby town of Cold Creek, Lyle Pettigrew was telling his cousins, Nutty and Deacon, that they were through waiting.

"But Jerry—" Deacon said.

"Jerry can come and find us," Lyle snapped. "We're not waitin' here until he decides he wants to join us."

"Where we goin'?" Nutty asked. "You got a bank picked out, Cousin?"

"Yeah, I got one picked out," he said. "We're gonna hit it and then get outta this godforsaken place."

"Cold Creek?"

"Cold Creek nothin'!" Lyle said. "Minnesota. Why didn't you tell me it was this cold?"

The other men didn't know who he was directing the question to, so they all remained silent.

"Never mind," he snapped. "Where's Joe?"

"He's still with that whore—"

"Fuck!" Lyle shouted, standing up. "He'd fuck till his dick fell off if I let him."

He charged up the stairs and down the hall to his brother's door, then kicked the door in. There was his brother, holding one of the whore's ankles in each hand, spreading her as far as she'd go, fucking her like a madman.

"Goddamnit, Joe!" he shouted.

He charged his brother, grabbed him by the shoulders, and not only pulled him off the girl, but off the bed as well.

Joe shouted, "Hey, what the—" as he hit the floor butt first. His baseball bat–sized prick quickly shriveled as he looked up at his brother.

"What the fuck—"

"You're gonna split the damn whore in two, damn it!" Lyle shouted.

"Well, ain't that the point?" Joe yelled back.

Lyle slapped his brother in the back of the head as hard as he could. Ever since Joe was a kid, that was the only way to get his attention.

"Pay the whore and get downstairs. We're gettin' ready to leave."

"I ain't finished."

Lyle looked at the girl on the bed. She'd curled up into a ball and was covering herself up. Lyle saw some blood on the sheets, but he couldn't tell where it was coming from. It wasn't a lot, though, so he figured he'd gotten to his brother before he could do much damage to the whore.

"Yeah, Joe," Lyle said, "you're finished. Deke, Nutty,

and me are waitin' downstairs. If you make me come up here again, I'm gonna hurt you. Understand?"

Joe Pettigrew was twice the size of his brother, but he ducked his head and said, "Yeah, Lyle, I understand."

Lyle turned and left the room.

NINETEEN

Nutty and Deacon looked up as the batwings opened and two men stepped in. They were both wearing badges.

"We're lookin' for Joe Pettigrew," one of them said.

His badge said "Sheriff" on it. The other, younger man's tin said "Deputy."

Nutty and Deacon looked at each other.

"Why you lookin' for him?" Lyle asked from the base of the steps.

The two men looked over at him.

"He's got a girl upstairs," the sheriff said. "Her friends are worried about her."

"Why?"

"Because he's had her for two days."

"Then he must like her."

"Look," the sheriff said, "we don't want no trouble. We just want the girl."

Lyle knew he could tell the two men they could have her, but he didn't like being told what to do.

"Are her friends whores, too?" he asked.

"That don't matter," the sheriff said.

"Look, Sheriff," Lyle said, "my brother will be done with her soon, and he'll send her home."

"In one piece?" the deputy asked.

Lyle looked at the younger man, whose hand was hovering over his gun.

"Son, you better relax that gun hand," he said. "I wasn't talkin' to you, I was talkin' to the sheriff."

"Well, I'm talkin' to—"

"Quiet, Mike."

"Yeah, shut up, Mike," Nutty said, and he and Deacon laughed.

The deputy flexed his gun hand.

"Sheriff," Lyle said, "this kid's liable to get you killed in the next five minutes."

"Nobody's gettin' killed, friend."

"Pettigrew," Lyle said, "my name's Lyle Pettigrew. These are my cousins, Nutty and Deacon."

"And Joe?"

"He's my brother."

"Is he upstairs?" the sheriff asked. "We'll just go up and get—"

Lyle held up his left hand.

"Nobody goes upstairs. My brother will be down directly."

"Get out of the way, Pettigrew!" the deputy said.

"Mike," the sheriff said warningly.

"You gonna let him tell us what to do, Sheriff?"

"That's just what I'm doin', Deputy," Lyle said. "I'm tellin' you what to do."

"Son of a—" the deputy said, going for his gun.

"Mike, no!" the sheriff shouted, but it was too late.

Nutty drew and shot the deputy in the chest. The young man coughed and dropped to the floor.

"Wait, wait—" the sheriff started shouting, but he was going for his gun at the same time.

Lyle drew and shot him in the chest. He fell over on top of the deputy.

"Damn, big brother!" Joe said. He was halfway down the stairs. "You're stackin' them like firewood."

"Shut up, Joe," Lyle said. "This is your fault."

The only other person in the room was the bartender, who was standing still behind the bar.

"Nutty, check on them," Lyle said.

Nutty walked to the two fallen lawmen, leaned over, and poked them.

"They're dead, Lyle."

"Fuck!" Lyle said. He turned around and looked up at his brother. "Joe—"

"Yeah, yeah, I know," Joe said. "It's my fault, right?"

"Damn right," Lyle said. "You and your whores are gonna get you killed one of these days. But I ain't about to let you get me killed, too."

"Well, none of us got killed," Joe said. "Just two lawmen."

He came down the stairs the rest of the way.

"Let's get somethin' to eat," he said.

"We'll eat on the trail," Lyle said. "We got to leave town."

"Why?" Joe asked.

"Because we killed two lawmen."

"But Jerry ain't here yet."

"Fuck Jerry!" Lyle said. "Nutty, you and Deke get the horses."

"Right."

"What about their pockets?" Joe asked, indicating the lawmen. "They might have some money."

"They're small-town lawmen, you idiot," Lyle said. "How much money would you get from them?"

"I don't know," Joe said. "Probably more than I have on me right now."

"Forget it!"

"Then what about a drink—"

"Just get out, Joe," Lyle said.

"But—"

"Out."

"Crap," Joe said, and stormed out of the saloon.

Lyle looked down at the two lawmen, then shrugged and decided to check their pockets. He got a total of three dollars. As an afterthought he took both their badges.

When he straightened up, his eyes fell on the bartender, who looked scared out of his mind.

"How much money you got?" he asked.

"Not a lot."

"Lemme see."

The bartender put the day's proceeds on the bar top. There was a dollar there, which Lyle had paid the man that morning. Since the Pettigrews had taken over the saloon, they hadn't been doing a lot of business.

Lyle took the dollar back.

"Sorry," he said to the bartender.

"That's okay," the man said. "Take it."

"No," Lyle said, "I'm sorry about this."

"Wha—"

Lyle drew his gun and shot the bartender in the chest. The man fell behind the bar.

"Can't leave any witnesses," Lyle said, and left.

TWENTY

"What's the next town?" Clint asked.

"Which way are you going?"

"Well, I've got to go south first. Hell, I might as well keep going south. It's too cold up here for me."

"You goin' back to the Gregory house?"

"Yes, I've got to tell her what happened. And I'd like to check on her, make sure she's okay. What happened to her husband?"

"His horse stepped into a chuck hole and fell on him," Walter Deadly said. "It was a freaky thing. Killed him instantly."

"She's been living out there alone for what? A year?" Clint asked.

"Little more. Wouldn't do her any good to move here. We got nothin' to offer her."

"Is there someplace else she could go?"

"Cold Creek, maybe."

"Where's that?"

"It's about as far from her house as we are, but farther south. In fact, you could ride there from here in the same amount of time. If you drew lines on a map from the house to here to Cold Creek and back, you'd have a triangle."

"Don't tell me," Clint said, "you used to be a teacher."

"Once upon a time."

They were sitting in the undertaker's office the morning after Clint had killed the two men. Clint had saddled Eclipse, and ridden over to tell the sheriff–undertaker that he was leaving. Walter Deadly was not sorry to see him go, even though he'd provided business for the man in both of his jobs.

"Guess I'll get going," Clint said, standing up. "What kind of town is Cold Creek?"

"Bigger than us," Deadly said. "Got a lawman and a deputy. Mrs. Gregory could do worse, I guess."

"I'll try to convince her."

Deadly walked Clint out to his horse.

"Sorry I made all that extra work for you," Clint said, mounting up.

"That's okay," Deadly said. He eyed the burlap sack hanging from Clint's saddle. "What's in the bag?"

"Just some supplies for Mrs. Gregory," Clint said. "Just in case I can't convince her to leave her house."

"Well, I wish you luck," Deadly said. "I've had some conversations with the woman and she's not easy to convince."

"Well, this experience may have changed her," Clint said. "I'll see if I can convince her."

Deadly held out his hand out and Clint shook it.

"I wish you luck," Deadly said. "If you get over to Cold Creek, give my best to the sheriff there, fella named Poulson. He's a good man."

"I'll tell him," Clint promised.

He turned Eclipse's head and rode out of town.

TWENTY-ONE

Clint pushed Eclipse and got to the Gregory house before the sun went down and it got any colder. He dismounted, approached the door, and then stepped back when it opened and Lori pointed a rifle at him. Her eyes were wide with fright.

"Lori, wait! It's me, Clint."

She stared at him and for a moment he thought she might shoot. Finally, she lowered the rifle as if it weighed a ton. Clint went to her and she fell into his arms. She looked like she hadn't slept in days.

"Oh God . . . ," she said as he helped her into the house and closed the door behind them.

He took the rifle from her and lowered her into a chair.

"Are you all right?" he asked.

"I think I'm going crazy," she said. "I haven't slept . . . I jump at every noise . . ."

Clint didn't think he was going to have much trouble convincing her to leave this house . . .

Clint made coffee after putting Lori to bed. She drifted right off to sleep now that he was there, and she needed it desperately. He sat down at the table with a cup of coffee and some beef jerky from his saddlebags. He didn't want to risk making noise by trying to cook something.

The poor woman had been living in a state of fear since he'd left. She even looked like she had lost weight since he'd last seen her. He needed to take her to a town—Cold Creek obviously—and get her to a doctor. He also hoped there would be some women there who could care for her. Once he brought her there, he wanted to head out, ride south and get away from the cold of Minnesota, and the bad luck of the place. He'd already had to kill three men, and he was still mighty curious about the first man, and whether or not he was related to the Pettigrews he'd heard about from Gloria two months ago in Kansas.

But that was then, this was now. He had to go out and see to Eclipse, get him bedded down and fed. He just hoped Lori wouldn't wake up while he was gone and panic. He hid the rifle, just in case.

When he came back in, his hands were frozen. He warmed them by the fireplace. Looking around, he didn't see anything in the little house that Lori Gregory couldn't do without. He'd seen an old saddle in the small barn. Hopefully, her horse would stay on its feet long enough to get her to Cold Creek.

He rolled himself up in his blanket in front of the fire and went to sleep.

He woke to the smell of bacon, rolled onto his back, and looked at Lori standing at the stove. He could hear the bacon sizzling. She was dressed, which included a riding skirt and boots.

"Where was that last time?" he asked.

"I guess I just wasn't in the mood," she called out. "You like it crisp?"

"So crisp it crumbles," he said.

"Biscuits?"

"If you've got them."

"Might as well cook what we've got," she said. She peered over her shoulder. "You are taking me away from here today, aren't you?"

He rolled over and got to his feet.

"I was going to try to convince you," he said.

"Oh, believe me," she said. "I'm convinced."

He stretched and walked over to the table. As he sat, she placed a cup of coffee in front of him, smiling at him. She was a different woman from the one who'd pointed a rifle at him the night before.

She opened the oven and took out the biscuits, removed the bacon from the frying pan, and set the whole thing on the table. Then she poured herself a cup of coffee and sat across from him.

"I want one biscuit and one slice of bacon," she said. "The rest is yours."

"No argument," he said.

He pulled the plate of bacon over to himself after she lifted a slice. There was butter on the plate with the biscuits. He cut one in half, buttered it, placed some bacon on it, and put it back together.

"Would you like some maple syrup for that?" she asked.

"This is fine, Lori," he said. "How are you today—or need I ask?"

"I didn't know if you'd ever come back," she said. "I decided if you did I was leaving with you."

"What if I don't want to take you?"

She smiled. "Why else would you have come back?"

He bit into the buttered biscuit, enjoying the crumble of the bacon.

"Good?" she asked.

"Perfect."

She looked calm—too calm.

"Are you packed?"

"Won't take but a minute."

"Do you care where you go?"

"Not really," she said. "Just as long as it's away from here."

"Oh, it will be," he said.

"I'll pack while you eat."

"I'll saddle the horses."

She stopped at the doorway to the other room.

"I hope we're not going too far," she said. "I don't know how long mine will last."

"Long enough," he said. "He's not much to look at, but he'll get you there."

"That's Rufus."

"Rufus?"

"My husband named him."

He nodded, buttered another biscuit, and said, "Go pack."

TWENTY-TWO

Lori took nothing more than a small garment bag. When she came out the front door, Clint helped her into the saddle, then handed the bag up to her.

"Can you ride?" he asked.

"Very well," she said, as he mounted up. "You won't have to wait up for me . . . but you might have to wait for Rufus. I don't think he can keep up to that monster of yours."

"We'll go easy—fast, but easy."

They started away from the house. She turned only once to look back at it.

"That was supposed to be our dream house," she said. "The dream died very quickly."

Clint turned and looked at her. He wondered if she remembered what had happened between them last time. She seemed more lucid this morning than he'd ever seen her.

"What's wrong?" she asked.

"Nothing," he said. "Nothing's wrong."

"Where are we going?" she asked.

"Cold Creek," he said. "You ever been there?"

"Once," she said. "We stopped there on our way to here."

"Why did your husband buy his supplies in Bedford, and not Cold Creek?"

"Bedford was closer."

"Not by much."

"He only had Rufus to get him there and back," she said. "So it was closer."

"Cold Creek is bigger, isn't it?"

"Lots."

Clint shrugged, and they rode for a while in silence. In fact, they rode all the way to Cold Creek.

Cold Creek was, indeed, larger than Bedford—a lot larger. Clint still wondered why her husband wouldn't have come here for his supplies. And then he started to wonder if maybe he did come here, but he told his bride he went to Bedford.

"Do you have any money?" he asked as they rode into town.

"Not a penny," she said.

"Okay," he said. "I'll put you in the hotel."

"And then what?"

"And then we'll talk," he said. "Let's get you situated first."

She pointed.

"That one will do."

It was a small hotel with the name "COLD CREEK" above the door. If there was another word after it, it had faded away a long time ago. This town was bigger than Bedford, but it didn't look much more prosperous.

"There might be a bigger hotel in town," he said.

"That one's good enough," she said.

"Okay."

After Lori was checked in, Clint left her in her room and took the horses to the livery stable. When he left, somebody called out, "Adams!"

He turned and saw Walter Deadly coming toward him.

"Well, which job brings you here, Deadly?" Clint said. "Undertaker or lawman?"

"A little of both, I'm afraid," Deadly said. "What are you doin' here?"

"I brought Lori Gregory here," Clint said. "Thought she needed to get away from that house."

"You might be right."

"What brings you here?"

"Remember I told you the sheriff here was a friend of mine?"

"Yes."

"Well, somebody killed him. I got the word soon after you left."

"Know who did it?"

Deadly nodded. "The Pettigrew gang."

"Pettigrew?"

"Apparently, the brothers and cousins of the one you killed."

"Pettigrews," Clint said again.

"Four of them."

"You going after them?"

"Soon as I can get up a posse," he said. "Looks like I'm gonna have to act like a real lawman for a while."

"I don't envy you."

"I was kinda glad to see you from across the street," he said.

Clint looked across the street. There was nothing there that would have interested Walter Deadly.

"Why was that, Mr. Deadly?"

"Just call me Walter, Adams."

"And I'm Clint."

"Clint, can I buy you a drink?"

"Sure, why not?"

"Saloon's this way."

TWENTY-THREE

"This town is five or six times the size of my town, Clint," Deadly said in the saloon. "And I swear, I could probably put a better posse together in Bedford than I can here."

"Then why don't you do it?"

"Because Bedford's in the other direction," Deadly said. "It would take too long. I need to build a posse here."

"Okay," Clint said, "make your pitch."

"I need you for this, Clint," he said. "Why? Because I've never done it before. I'm determined to hunt these men down because they killed a lawman, a lawman who happened to be my friend. There's only one problem."

"What's that?"

"I don't know how to do it."

"Don't you have any deputies in town?"

"There was one," Deadly said. "They killed him, too."

"Nobody else?"

"I've got men who want to ride," Deadly said, "but they're likely to get themselves killed, and me, too."

"Your pitch, Walter."

"I want you to ride with the posse," Deadly said. "Actually, I want you to lead it, but it has to look like I'm leading it. Do you understand?"

"I understand the request, Walter."

"But will you do it?"

"You're not making it sound very attractive," Clint said. "You want me to lead a posse of trigger-happy men and make it look like an inexperienced lawman is doing it. Can I do all that and stay alive?"

"I hope you can," Deadly said. "If you get killed, I'll be stuck out there alone."

"With a bunch of trigger-happy townsmen."

"You have to do this, Clint," Deadly said. "If just to keep me alive."

"Well, Walter," Clint said, "I'm going to do it, but I have other reasons than keeping you alive."

"Like what?"

"Well, I've got to find out if Pettigrew is a common name."

"What?"

"And I need to find out if I'm involved in a coincidence," Clint said, "because I hate coincidences."

"What are you talking about?"

"I first heard the name Pettigrew a couple of months ago," Clint said. "I want to find out if these are the same ones."

"I don't know what that means," Deadly said, "but are you riding with the posse?"

"I'll ride with your posse, Walter," Clint said. "Just remember, it's your posse."

"Okay, Clint," Sheriff Deadly said. "Okay. Let's have one more beer on it."

"Bring it on."

Clint turned while Deadly ordered two more beers. At that moment the batwing doors opened and a woman walked in. She was wearing trail clothes and a gun on her hip. She attracted the attention of the other men in the saloon, which, at that time of the evening, was busy as hell.

She looked familiar to Clint as she studied the room.

Deadly turned and handed Clint a beer. At that moment the woman looked over at them and then started toward them.

"You're the sheriff?" she asked Deadly.

"That's right, miss."

"I want to volunteer," she said.

"Volunteer for what?" Deadly asked.

"The posse," she said. "You are putting together a posse, aren't you?"

"Well, yeah, but—"

"I want to ride with you."

"Ma'am," Deadly asked, "have you ever ridden with a posse?"

"No."

"Have you ever killed a man?"

"Yes, I have."

That stopped Deadly. "You have?"

"Yes."

"Who?"

"A man named Pettigrew."

There was that name again. "Hello, Gloria," Clint said.

She looked at Clint, seeing him for the first time. "Clint Adams?"

"How are you, Gloria?"

"I'm fine," she said. "What are you doin' here?"

"I'm riding with the posse," he said. "We're going after a gang named Pettigrew."

"I know that."

"There's four of them."

"Four?" she said. "There used to be six. I killed one of them."

"And I killed one of them," he said.

"Well," Deadly said, "if you know this young lady and she's already killed a member of the Pettigrew gang, I guess she should come along."

"Thank you, Sheriff. When will we be leaving?"

"First thing in the morning, Miss . . ."

"Mundy," she said, "Gloria Mundy. Just call me Gloria, Sheriff."

"All right, Gloria," he said. "Would you like to have a beer?"

"No, sir," she said. "I just got to town and I need to get a hotel room."

"I know a nice small hotel, Gloria," Clint said. "Why don't I walk you there?"

"All right, Clint."

"But I want to finish this beer first," he said. "Why don't you have one, too?"

"Well . . . all right," she said. "I guess one won't hurt. I am pretty hungry, though."

"After the beer we'll get you a room, and then we'll have something to eat and catch up," Clint said. "I want you to explain to me how this whole coincidence happened."

"I'll do my best," she said.

TWENTY-FOUR

Clint ended up with both Gloria Mundy and Lori Gregory in a small café down the street from the hotel. They all had steak dinners in front of them.

Clint had checked Gloria into a room at the hotel and then had taken her to Lori's room so they could meet. The two women seemed to get along immediately, although he wasn't sure why—even though they were very close in age.

"I don't understand, Gloria," Lori said. "Why would you want to ride with the posse?"

"The Pettigrews killed my family," Gloria said. "I'm going to kill them."

"Why don't you leave that to Clint?" she asked. "He's already killed one of them."

"So have I," Gloria said. "I've tracked them for hundreds of miles, and I've killed one of them. And I intend to kill the rest."

"Well," Lori said, "if you're that committed to it . . ."

"You could come, too," Gloria said. "Did they kill somebody in your family?"

"No," Lori said, "my husband died from a fall . . . a stupid fall. No, all Jerry Pettigrew did was . . . rape me for five days."

Gloria stared across the table at her.

"And you don't want to kill that whole family?" she asked.

"Well . . . the one who raped me is dead, thanks to Clint. I think I could have killed him if I had the chance, but . . . I don't think I could ride with a posse. I mean, I don't wear a gun like a man . . . like you do. I . . . I admire you, Gloria."

"Don't admire me," Gloria said. "I'm driven by hate. It burns inside me, and nothin' is gonna put it out but killin' that whole family."

"You say you killed one of them already?" Clint asked.

"I left Jasper, Kansas, soon after you did," she said. "I started tracking them. It wasn't hard. They were leaving a lot of bodies behind them. I finally found one of them—his name was Lemuel—in an Arizona whorehouse, and killed him."

"With a gun?" Lori asked.

"Yes," she said. "I caught him with his pants down, and his gun belt hanging on the bedpost. He went for it, but I beat him."

"I don't think I could've done that," Lori said.

"I had a good teacher," Gloria said, "and my hate is still as hot as ever."

Clint walked back to the hotel with both women, left Gloria at her room first, then walked Lori to hers.

"She's an amazing girl," Lori said.

"Yes, she is."

"Do you think I'm weak because I couldn't kill anyone?"

"I don't think you're weak at all, Lori."

"But I left my home," she said. "I left because I was frightened to stay alone."

"I think it took a lot of strength to leave home, Lori."

"Do you really?"

"Yes."

She opened her door, hesitated in the doorway, then turned to look at him. Once again he wondered what, if anything, she remembered from the first night he'd spent in her house.

"So you'll be leaving tomorrow to ride with the posse?" she asked.

"Looks like it."

"And Gloria's goin', too?"

"Yes."

"Do you know when you'll be back?"

"No," he said, "but I'll pay for your room for a week ahead. You'll have that long to decide what you want to do."

"I should get a job," she said.

"Probably."

"Except I ain't never had one before."

"I'm sure you'll be able to find something."

"Maybe sewin'," she said. "I can sew."

"You'll have time to decide."

"Well . . . ," she said, "good night."

"Good night, Lori."

Clint waited until she had closed the door and locked it. Then he walked down the hall to his room, which was around the corner and next to Gloria's. He unlocked the door and entered, then stopped when he saw Gloria in his bed.

"Well," she said, smiling, "I'm glad you didn't bring Lori back here with you."

TWENTY-FIVE

"Why would you think I'd bring her back here?" Clint asked.

Gloria was nestled in the crook of his left arm. He had wasted no time joining her in the bed, and they had spent the better part of an hour getting reacquainted.

"Can't you tell?" she asked. "The girl's in love with you."

"That's ridiculous."

"Is it? Tell me you haven't been with her."

"That was . . . different."

"How?"

"She thought I was her dead husband."

"What?" Gloria pushed herself up so she could look directly at him.

"She was in shock, and thought I was her husband."

"And you took advantage of her in that condition?" she demanded.

"No, of course not."

"But you did have sex with her?"

"Yes, but—"

She sat up and stared at him, arms folded across her naked breasts.

"This should be good."

He took the time to explain to her in detail what had happened to Lori, and what had occurred after he saved her from Jerry Pettigrew.

When he was finished, she stared at him and said, "Well, you did it."

"Did what?"

"You managed to explain it away," she said. "What you did was . . . wonderful."

"Well, I don't know if it was wonderful."

She lay back down next him, plastering the length of her body to his.

"I still think she's in love with you, though."

"Despite what you think, every woman who meets me doesn't fall in love with me."

"I didn't say that!" she said, pinching some skin on his side. "I hope you don't think that I'm in love with you."

"You're not?"

"Of course not," she said. "I have too much hate in me to love anybody, don't you think?"

"Gloria—"

"No, don't try to talk me out of it," she said. "I'm only kiddin' slightly. I know what hate can do, Clint. I'm not a fool."

"If you gave up your quest," he said, "you could—"

"No," she said, cutting him off. "Don't try it, Clint. I'm not givin' up. I'll be leavin' with that posse tomorrow mornin'."

"All right," he said. "If that's what you want."

They got quiet then for a while, and just when he thought she might have fallen asleep, she asked, "What are you thinkin'?"

"I was just . . . ah, I was thinking maybe I could've made more of a difference when we first met."

"How so?"

"I could have tried to talk you out of this back then," he said, "or I could have gone with you."

"You couldn't have done either one," she told him.

"Maybe . . ."

"No," she said, "I was determined then, and there was no way you could give up your life to follow my path. I knew that then, and I know it now."

"But here we are," he said, "riding in the same posse, chasing the Pettigrews."

"It's just a coincidence."

"A coincidence?" he said. "No, more like fate has brought me back around to do what I should have done in the first place."

"You hate coincidences that much?" she asked. "You can't just admit that this is one?"

"No," he said, "I can't."

"Well," she said, "whatever it is that's brought us together to do this, I'm glad."

"I am, too," he said. "If we can get the rest of them all at once, you'll be free to get on with your life."

After a moment she said, "That will be . . . hard. I don't even know what I'll do when I don't have this hate to keep me warm."

"It doesn't keep you warm, Gloria," he said. "That's cold you feel, not warmth. Once it's gone, you'll be free to be a warm and loving woman."

"Loving?" she asked. "You mean, fall in love with a man?"

"Why not?"

"I don't have much faith in men, Clint," she said. "You're the only one I've ever known who's worth anything."

"What about your father?" he asked.

"My father used to beat me and my mother," she said.

"Then why are you so determined to avenge his death?" Clint asked.

"Because he was my father," she said.

Oddly, Clint thought that he probably understood that.

* * *

Clint woke first the next morning. Gloria had stayed the night with him, instead of going back to her own room. It wasn't yet light out, but it was close to first light.

He slid his arm out from beneath her, got out of bed, and walked to the window. The street was quiet, but he knew the posse would soon be forming. He wondered how many men Walter Deadly had managed to gather.

"Is it time?" Gloria asked from the bed.

"Close," he said.

"I should go back to my room and get ready."

He swung his legs around and sat on the edge of the bed, naked.

"Unless you've got a reason why I should stay?" she asked.

"I've got a lot of reasons," he said, "but if we're going with that posse, we'd better start getting ready now."

"Okay," she said, standing up. "Your loss."

He stared at her as she padded naked to the door.

"I know it is," he said.

She smiled, put on her robe, and slipped out the door.

TWENTY-SIX

Clint met Gloria in the lobby of the hotel. As they stepped outside, the first beam of sunlight broke through and lit their way to the livery stable, where they saddled their horses. When they rode their horses over to the sheriff's office, they saw a group of men and horses gathered out front.

"It looks like the sheriff got a few men to go with him," Gloria said.

Clint nodded. It looked like almost a dozen men milling about in the street.

As they reached the group, the door to the sheriff's office opened and Walter Deadly stepped out. The attention of the posse members was split between Deadly and Gloria Mundy.

"What the hell—" one of them said, and others screwed up their faces in puzzlement.

"A woman?" one of them said aloud.

"Sheriff, what the hell—"

"What's a woman doin' here?"

"Settle down," Deadly called out. "This lady has more of a right to be a member of this posse than the rest of you. The Pettigrews killed her whole family in Kansas."

"That might be," a man said, "but I don't wanna get killed because some girl is not pullin' her weight."

"Don't worry, mister," Gloria said. "I'll pull my weight. I've already killed one of them."

"Is that true?" another man asked.

"Yes," the sheriff said. "She's been tracking this gang and has killed one of them. Also, Clint Adams has killed one."

"Adams!" someone called out, shocked.

"That's me," Clint said.

"The Gunsmith is ridin' with this posse?" the first man asked.

"Mr. Adams has agreed to ride with us, since he's already had experience with one of the gang."

"And what about you, Sheriff?" another voice asked. "Ain't you the undertaker from over ta Bedford?"

"I am the undertaker," Deadly said, "but I'm also the sheriff."

"Sheriff named Deadly?" someone said, laughing. "I hope you live up to your name."

"Well, that just means we can kill 'em and bury 'em at the same time."

The posse started to laugh, all but Deadly, Clint, and Gloria.

Clint looked over at Deadly. If the man lost control of the posse now, he'd never be able to regain their respect. He thought about stepping in, but that wouldn't have been helpful.

He watched as Deadly drew his gun and fired a round into the boardwalk at his feet. The laughing abruptly stopped.

"This is no laughing matter!" he snapped. "Anybody who thinks this posse is gonna be fun can leave right now!"

The ten or twelve men exchanged glances, but only two of them—right upfront, side by side—laughed and elbowed each other. To Clint, they also looked drunk.

"What's your name?" Deadly asked one of them.

"Me? I'm Ed Winston."

"And you?" Deadly asked the other.

"Paul Nichols."

Deadly walked up between their horses, inspected their saddlebags, then suddenly reached into one.

"Hey!" Nichols shouted.

Deadly came out with a bottle of whiskey that was about half-full.

"Seems to me you both been nippin' at this," Deadly said. "Clint, you think you can take care of this for me?"

"I think Gloria can, Sheriff."

Deadly looked at Clint to be sure he'd heard right, then shrugged and tossed the bottle into the air. Gloria drew and fired. At its apex the bullet caught the bottle and shattered it. Glass and whiskey rained down over the men.

In that split second both Walter Deadly and Gloria Mundy earned the respect of the men.

"You two are out," Deadly said to Nichols and Winston."

"You can't do—" Ed Winston started, but Deadly cut him off.

"Anybody here want to ride after the Pettigrew gang with a couple of drunks?"

The other men shook their heads, and several of them shouted, "No!"

"That's it," Deadly said to the two men again. "You're out. The rest of you, we'll be leaving in ten minutes. You." Deadly pointed to the youngest member of the group, a man in his early twenties who had been staring at Gloria the whole time. "Go over to the livery. The fella there will show you my horse and saddle. Saddle 'im up and bring him over here for me."

"Yessir."

The young man tossed one last look at Gloria and then rode to the livery.

The two men ousted from the posse turned their horses and grudgingly rode away.

"Clint? Can I see you inside?" Deadly asked.

Clint nodded, dismounted, and handed his reins to Gloria. As he followed Deadly into the office, he heard someone say, "That was mighty good shootin', little lady," and a few others agreed.

Inside the office Deadly turned to Clint and expelled a breath he might have holding the whole time.

"Did you know she'd make that shot?" he asked.

"I was hoping."

"Hoping?"

"I had a pretty good idea she would," Clint said. "It's a good thing you can spot a drunk."

"That wasn't hard," Deadly said. "Half the folks at a funeral are already liquored up."

"Well, I think you managed to get some respect, for now."

"There were ten men out there. Now we got eight."

"Eleven when you add us in."

"That a good size for a posse?"

"I'd say it's a little big," Clint said. "By the end of the day, though, some of them will turn back. Others will stay with you for a couple of days. In the end we might end up with half a dozen of us, but they'll be men—and one woman—who want to do the job."

"You should know the Pettigrews have about a four-day head start on us," Deadly said.

"They could be across the state line already, Sheriff," Clint said. "What happens then?"

"I intend to chase them until I catch them," Deadly said.

Clint had to admit that when he met Walter Deadly, the undertaker, he had not expected to ever find this kind of determination in him.

"I know what you're thinkin'," Deadly said, "but like I told you, Zack Poulson was my friend. He'd been the sheriff here for three years."

"How did he get killed?"

"From what I hear his deputy, Mike Hogan, went for his gun and got both of them killed. Then they killed the bartender for good measure."

"Any idea which way they headed after they left here?" Clint asked.

"Somebody said they heard them talkin' about goin' south, to get out of the cold."

"Can't say I blame them for that."

"Due south of here is the town of Cottonwood. According to the sheriff there, the Pettigrews passed through a day ago."

"One day?" Clint said. "I thought we were three days behind them?"

"Cottonwood's fifty miles from here," Deadly said. "They must've found some trouble between here and there that held them up."

"Well," Clint said, "I guess a one-day head start could be worse."

"There are some homesteads, and some small towns—mud puddles really—between us and Cottonwood," Deadly explained. "We should be able to find out something between here and there."

"Only if we get going," Clint said.

Deadly walked to the gun rack, grabbed a shotgun, and said, "I'm ready."

Clint hoped Walter Deadly really was ready.

TWENTY-SEVEN

Halfway between Cold Creek and Cottonwood the posse found out what the Pettigrews had been up to.

Clint and Deadly had decided they had one man in the posse who might have been worth the posse fee he was getting. His name was Miller Lastings, and he seemed to have some tracking abilities. Unlike the other members, he was not a shopkeeper looking to get away from his business for a while, or a husband looking to get away from his wife.

Deadly had sent Lastings on ahead to scout. They expected the Pettigrew gang to be south of Cottonwood by now, and probably in the state of Iowa, but they didn't want any surprises.

Lastings had been riding ahead of them for about three hours when he appeared in the distance, riding hell-bent-for-leather back to them.

"Hold up," Deadly said, raising his hand. "Let's see what Lastings is so excited about."

The riders stopped and waited for Lastings to reach them.

"What's the matter?" Deadly asked.

"There's a ranch up ahead," Lastings said. "You better come."

"What is it?" Deadly asked again.

"Looks like the Pettigrew gang burned these people out—and killed everyone. From the looks of things, they took their time about it."

"Oh God," Gloria said.

"Maybe the lady would like to skip this part and head back—" Lastings started.

"Don't start that!" Gloria snapped, pointing at the man.

"Sorry," he muttered.

"Okay, Lastings," Deadly said. "Lead the way."

Lastings turned and started off at a gallop, and the posse followed.

Lastings had a good pony, which started to put some distance between him and the posse—everyone but Clint. Eclipse was able to easily keep up with the animal, and could have passed it if need be. But Lastings was leading the way, so Clint stayed right with him.

Soon enough they came within sight of the burned-out ranch. As they got closer, Clint spotted a couple of bodies lying on the ground.

Lastings and Clint reined in their horses and dismounted. The rest of the posse would be there in minutes.

"See what I mean?" Lastings asked.

Clint walked to the two bodies. They were both men, and they had been shot, not burned to death. There was a corral nearby with two horses in it.

"Near as I can figure from the tracks, there were four riders. Looks like they rested their horses. In fact, I think the two horses in the corral belonged to them. They must have taken two fresh mounts."

Clint walked over to the corral to have a look. One of the horses was limping.

"Doesn't figure they'd have to rest their horses after riding here from Cottonwood," he said. "But that one looks lame."

"There's also this," Lastings said, pointing toward the house.

"What?"

"There are bodies in the rubble."

"How many?"

"I took a quick look," Lastings said. "I found two women."

"Women?"

"Well, maybe a girl and a woman."

"Christ," Clint said, as the rest of the posse reached them and reined in.

"What do we have?" Deadly asked.

"Bodies," Clint said. "Two men shot to death, at least two females in the fire. I was just going to take a look."

"Yeah, let's take a look," one of the posse said.

Clint pulled Deadly aside.

"We don't need everybody stomping around in there."

"Gotcha." Deadly turned and said, "Everybody stay where you are. Adams and I are gonna take a look." He looked at Lastings. "You stay here, too."

"Fine with me," Lastings said. "I've seen more than enough."

Clint and Walter Deadly moved into the rubble of the burned out house. They found the two females Lastings mentioned. The house had been a large one, with several rooms. As they moved about, they found other bodies—another female and two male who both appeared to be small children. There were also a lot of empty whiskey bottles lying about.

They could tell that the clothing of the third female they found had been torn off of her.

"Looks like they took over this house, got drunk, probably raped the women, and killed the men," Sheriff Deadly said.

"And a couple of boys," Clint added.

Deadly put his hands on his hips and shook his head. "I want these men, Clint."

"I feel the same way," Clint said, "but it looks like we've got some graves to dig first."

"That'll hold us up," Deadly said, "but there's no way to avoid it."

"Let's get everyone on it," Clint said. "It'll go faster that way."

Deadly walked back to the posse and called out that everybody was going to have to start digging some graves. He told Lastings to water all the horses while the rest of the posse was digging. He included Gloria in the grave digging.

Clint kept walking through the rubble, showing the posse members the bodies of the two boys they had found.

Once they'd carried all the bodies out and laid them on the ground with the two men, they started digging graves—seven of them.

TWENTY-EIGHT

After they buried the seven family members, the posse went back to their horses. The men drank from their canteens, then refilled them at a nearby well. Clint, Deadly, and Gloria stood off to one side.

"They spent some time here," Clint said. "They might have been trying to work on that lame horse, but finally gave up and just took what horses these people had."

"After torturing, raping, and killing them," Gloria said. "There were two little boys in there."

"I know," Clint said.

Deadly looked at the sky.

"If we push, we can still make Cottonwood tonight," he said. "We might come up with some more information there."

"You know the sheriff there?" Clint asked.

"I don't," Deadly said, "but I'm sure Zack Poulson must've known him. If he knew Zack, he'll want to help."

"We better get moving then," Clint said.

Miller Lastings came over and said, "Sheriff, some of the men want to turn back."

"Already?" Deadly said, looking at Clint.

"This is what happens with posses," Clint said. "They've

seen what the Pettigrews can do. They have families back in town."

Deadly rubbed his jaw. "Guess I can't blame them then."

"Well, I can," Gloria said. "It's because they have families that they should stay with it. They're just . . . cowards."

"I'll talk to them," Deadly said.

As he walked away with Lastings, Gloria said to Clint, "He's gonna let them go?"

"He can't make them stay with the posse, Gloria," Clint said.

"Anybody who tries to turn back should be shot," she said.

"I guess I'm glad you're not wearing the badge here," Clint replied.

"Don't you agree?"

"No, Gloria, I don't," he said. "I really don't want to be in a posse with a bunch of men who don't want to be there."

"I . . . I guess you're right."

Deadly came back.

"Four of them are turning back," he said. "The married ones."

"That figures."

"Two more will quit when we get to Cottonwood, I think," Deadly said. "The kid will stay, and probably Lastings. We'll end up a posse of five."

"When we tell the people in Cottonwood what happened to this family, maybe we'll get some volunteers," Clint said. "They'll probably know who this family was."

"Yeah," Deadly said. "Probably."

"Maybe the sheriff and his deputies will come along," Gloria offered.

"Well," Deadly said, "we won't know until we get there, and we won't get there if we stand here yapping away. I'll get 'em mounted."

"Five of us," Gloria said to Clint. "That's plenty. There's only four of them."

"Four killers," Clint said. "The kid and Lastings, they're not killers."

"And the sheriff?"

"Not really," Clint said, "but he's wearing the badge, so he'll do the job."

"So that leaves you and me."

"Don't kid yourself, Gloria," he said. "You're no killer."

"But I'll kill them," she said.

"Yes," he said, "I know you will. Come on, let's get mounted up."

TWENTY-NINE

The posse rode into Cottonwood after dark. Deadly gave Miller Lastings his horse to put up in the livery and told the posse members to get themselves a meal and some place to stay.

"Is the town paying for the rooms?" one of the posse members asked.

"Pay for your own damn room!" Gloria snapped.

"You got no call to talk to me like that," the man said.

"Oh no? We'll see if you ride out with us in the morning," she said, "then I'll decide if I have a right to talk to you like that."

"Pay for the room, Lee," Deadly said. "You'll get your money back when we get back to Cold Creek—your room and your meal."

"Okay, Sheriff."

"Hey, kid, what's your name?" Clint asked the youngest member of the posse.

"Me? I'm Caleb, Mr. Adams."

"Caleb, take this money," Clint said, "and take my horse to the livery, will you? Make sure he's well taken care of."

"Yes, sir."

"Don't try to pet him, or ride him," Clint warned. "He might take a finger off."

"Uh, yessir."

"Then you and Gloria go and get something to eat."

"Wha—me and Gloria?"

He pulled the boy aside.

"I just want you to look out for her, okay? Keep her out of trouble. I'm going to go with the sheriff to talk to the local law."

"Uh, okay, sure, yessir."

"Good. Here." He gave the boy Eclipse's reins. "Wait for Gloria."

He went over to her.

"What are you doin'?" she asked.

"He's just a kid," he said. "Keep an eye on him. I think he's going to stay with us."

"Me keep an eye on him, right?"

"That's right. Here." He gave her some money. "Get yourself a room and something to eat. I'll see you later."

He caught up to Deadly, who was heading for the sheriff's office.

"What'd you do?" Deadly asked.

"I got the two of them to watch out for each other."

"Not a bad idea. She seems to be getting a little hot under the collar."

"Yeah," Clint said, "maybe babysitting will help cool her off."

Cottonwood was clearly a larger town than Cold Creek. In fact, it was the biggest town Clint had seen since getting to Minnesota.

"Yeah, it's the county seat," Deadly said, when Clint mentioned that.

"Is there a marshal here?" Clint asked.

"Just the sheriff," Deadly said. "His jurisdiction is the whole county."

"So if the Pettigrews were here, why didn't he do something?"

"They didn't break any laws here," Deadly said. "In fact, they're not wanted in Minnesota—at least, they weren't. They will be now that we found that massacred family."

Clint had his doubts, since nobody had actually seen the Pettigrews kill the family and burn their home, but he didn't say anything to Deadly. And he suddenly had a bad feeling about getting help from the county sheriff.

THIRTY

When they entered the sheriff's office, there were three men there—one behind a desk, the other two in front. They were all wearing badges.

"Help ya?" one of them asked. His badge said "Deputy."

"I'm lookin' for the sheriff," Deadly said.

"That's me," the older man behind the desk said. "Sheriff Cal Shepherd. Boys, give these gents some room."

The two deputies backed off. Clint and Deadly could have sat, but they chose not to.

"I'm Walter Deadly," Deadly said, "sheriff over in Bedford."

"Bedford?" one of the deputies said. "Ain't that nothin' but a mud hole?"

"Wait a minute," the other deputy said, pointing at Deadly. "You're the undertaker there, right?"

"That's right," Deadly said, showing his badge, "undertaker and sheriff."

"Undertaker and sheriff," one of the deputies repeated, and the two young men started nudging each other.

"Okay, you two, out," Sheriff Shepherd said.

"Hey, Sheriff—"

"Go on, get out and make your rounds."

The two men picked up their hats, and were still nudging each other and laughing as they went out the door.

"You should teach your deputies some respect," Clint said. "If not for the man, for the badge."

Shepherd, a man in his fifties who had kept himself in good shape, looked at Clint. "And you are?"

"I'm Clint Adams," Clint said, "but that doesn't matter. Sheriff Deadly here has some business to discuss with you."

"Business?" Shepherd said. Then recognition dawned. "Hey, you're the Gunsmith."

"That's right," Deadly said, "he's the Gunsmith, and he's ridin' with me and my posse."

"Posse?"

"From Cold Creek."

"Cold Creek? Sheriff Poulson with you?"

"Zack is dead."

That stopped the sheriff in his tracks.

"Zack Poulson is dead?"

"Him and his deputy. I sent a telegram asking you about the Pettigrew gang?"

"Pettigrew gang," Shepherd repeated. "I never heard of them. There were some men in town named Pettigrew a couple days ago, but I had no paper on them. And they didn't break any laws while they were here."

"There's a family lives about twenty-five miles north of here? You know them?"

"The Forresters? Sure. Husband, wife, four kids."

"There was seven people."

"Oh yeah, the wife's brother. He lives with them, too."

"Lived with them," Deadly said. "They're all dead, and their place was burned to the ground."

"Dead? All of them?"

"Yes."

Shepherd looked at Clint. He nodded.

"Killed by the Pettigrews?"

"Yes," Deadly said.

"Witnesses?"

"They were all dead."

"Then how do you know these men did it?"

"I know."

"Look . . . Sheriff . . . you can't just know, you have to be able to prove it."

"Well, when my posse and me catch 'em, I'll prove it. But I need your help."

"My help? How?"

"Did you talk to them while they were here?"

"Briefly, just to find out what they were doing in town, how long they were staying."

"And how long was that?"

"Just overnight."

"Any idea where they were headed?"

"South," he said. "They wanted to get away from the cold."

"Look," Deadly said, "they killed the Forresters, they killed Zack Poulson and his deputy—"

"And you have witnesses to that?"

"Well . . . no. They also killed the bartender, who would've been a witness."

"Then you've got nothing on these men that you can prove."

"They killed a family in Kansas," Clint said.

"When?"

"Years ago."

"Then they're wanted in Kansas," Shepherd said, "not here."

"You and your deputies can ride with us," Deadly said.

"I can't leave here."

"Then you can loan me your deputies."

"They can't leave either. Besides, these Pettigrews are over the border by now. You can't go after them."

"But I am," Deadly said. "Zack was my friend, and that family deserves to be avenged."

"There, you see?" Shepherd said.

"See what?"

"You don't know what it means to wear that badge," Shepherd said. "Our job is not about vengeance, it's about justice."

"Then they deserve justice."

Shepherd leaned back in his chair.

"You should go back to Bedford, Mr. Deadly," Shepherd said. "Go back to being an undertaker. I'm sure you're very good at that."

"You're not gonna help at all?"

"Why should I?" Shepherd asked. "You've got the famous Gunsmith at your side."

"You're not really one to be telling Sheriff Deadly his job, Sheriff."

"And who are you to try to tell me mine, Adams?" Shepherd demanded.

"Two lawmen have been killed," Clint said. "Don't you think that deserves a little rule breaking?"

"I don't break the rules," Shepherd said. "I don't even bend them."

"I find that very easy to believe."

"You come at me with some evidence, and you'll see me do my job."

"Thanks for your help . . . Sheriff." Deadly turned and left, with Clint following.

"I may run against that son of a bitch in the next election," Deadly said with feeling.

"I'll move here just to vote for you," Clint said. "You want to get a steak?"

"A steak and a beer."

"Let's find a place."

They were still looking when they saw Gloria and the kid sitting in the window of a small restaurant.

"Want to join them?" Clint asked.

"Why not?"

They went inside and walked to the table. The window bothered Clint, so he sat down so that he could see out clearly.

"What happened?" Gloria asked after the waiter took Clint and Deadly's order.

"You want to tell them?" Clint asked Deadly.

"No, you tell them," Deadly said. "I get madder the more I think about it."

THIRTY-ONE

"So he's not gonna help," Gloria said. "That's no big surprise. I've been running into that attitude ever since I started hunting them."

"It doesn't sound fair," the kid said.

"Nothin' is fair, Caleb," she told him. "You have to learn that." She looked at Clint and Deadly. "So what do we do now?"

"I know what I'm gonna do," Deadly said. "I'm gonna track those men until I catch them."

"I'm with you, Sheriff," Gloria said.

"So am I," Caleb said. From the way he was looking at Gloria, Clint thought he knew why he was sticking around. Clint only hoped the kid wouldn't shoot himself in the foot . . . or worse.

"If we can find Lastings, I think he'll stick with us, too," Deadly said.

"Better find him before he gets too drunk," Caleb said.

"Why?" Clint asked. "What do you know?"

The kid shrugged.

"I know that Lastings likes to get drunk at night," he said simply. "You'll find him where there are girls, and whiskey."

"You better go and find him, Caleb," Clint said. "See if you can convince him not to get drunk."

"We'll want to start out at first light," Deadly said.

"What about the others?" Caleb asked, getting to his feet.

"I'm pretty sure it'll just be the five of us," Deadly said. "Unless somebody else wants to turn back?"

"Not me," Gloria said.

"Me neither," Caleb said.

"Go," Clint said to Caleb.

"If Gloria comes with me, we can keep each other out of trouble."

Clint looked at Gloria.

"Why not?" she said with a shrug. "It's somethin' to do."

She left the restaurant with Caleb happily following her.

"The kid's in love," Deadly said.

"He's going to be disappointed."

"Aren't we all when we fall in love?"

"At one time or another, yes."

The waiter brought them their steaks and they attacked them with gusto.

"Let's get a drink," Deadly said as they left the restaurant half an hour later.

"Why not?"

They started toward a saloon they could see from their vantage point.

"Posses," Clint said. "I've never been part of one that just got the job done. There's always something."

"It's much easier dealing with the dead," Deadly said. "They just lie there and wait for you to be finished with them."

"You could do what Sheriff Shepherd suggested, and go back to Bedford and just be an undertaker for a while."

"I intend to do that," he answered, "after we catch the Pettigrews."

They reached the saloon and entered. It was mobbed, but they were able to find elbow room for two men at the bar. When they each had a beer, they turned to take in the scene. The room was very large, with high ceilings and very ornate furnishings. There were at least half a dozen girls working the floor. There was a piano in the corner, but at the moment no one was playing it.

"You can't blame the sheriff," Clint said. "He does need evidence to act."

"He's rigid," Deadly said. "Men who won't bend usually break, at some point. I've put a lot of them into the ground."

"We can get this done, Sheriff," Clint said. "It may take days, or weeks, or even months, and a lot of miles, but we can do it."

"With a drunk, a kid, and a woman?"

"The woman can shoot. I think you helped prove that yourself," Clint said. "And don't forget she's already killed one of them. And Lastings did okay yesterday. Our only real question mark is the kid."

"Not exactly," Deadly said. "I'm afraid I may be the biggest question mark of all."

"Well," Clint said, "I guess we'll get all our questions answered when we catch up to them."

Deadly nodded and sighed.

"I just hope we get the answers I want."

THIRTY-TWO

Clint woke in the morning, came down to the lobby, and found the kid, Caleb, waiting there.

"Good morning," he said.

"Mornin', Mr. Adams. Are we goin' now?"

"Soon, kid, soon," Clint said. "I need some breakfast first. I think we all do."

"Count me in," Deadly said, coming up behind Clint. He looked at Caleb. "Where's Lastings?"

"He found a girl last night, took her to his room," Caleb said. "He promised he wouldn't get drunk, and that he'd meet us this morning."

"And I guess he kept his promise," Clint said as Lastings entered the lobby.

"Breakfast anyone?" he asked. "I found a really good place for it."

"We just need to wait for Gloria," Clint said.

"I can wait," Caleb said. "Or I could go up and knock on her door—"

"Nobody needs to knock on my door," Gloria said, coming down the stairs. "I'm here and I'm hungry."

"Then let's go," Clint said. "Lastings, lead the way."

* * *

He took them to a small café, blocks from the one where Clint and Deadly had eaten their steaks. Clint went for steak and eggs, Deadly the same. Around the table bacon or ham and eggs were called for. The waitress returned with two pots of coffee.

"So it's just us?" Lastings asked.

"Looks that way," Deadly said.

"Ah, we can handle it, right, kid?"

"That's right," Caleb said.

"Lastings, after we eat, why don't you and Caleb go and fetch the horses. Clint, Gloria, and me will go to the general store and get some supplies."

"Let's travel light," Clint said. "Enough to keep us alive and warm, but not enough to need a packhorse."

"Suits me," Deadly said. "I'd rather travel light and fast."

The waitress brought their plates, and they all started eating.

During the meal Deadly told them all that they were probably going to be crossing state lines, if that mattered to anyone.

"That's only gonna matter to you, Sheriff," Lastings said. "You're the only one that's official."

"I just want you all to know I'm committed to running these men down no matter how long it takes."

"So am I," Gloria said.

"I got nothin' better to do," Lastings said.

"Me neither," Caleb said.

"So we're all committed," Clint said. "Now we just need to pick up their trail."

"That won't be hard," Gloria said. "They pretty much leave a trail of bodies behind them wherever they go."

"Once they cross into Iowa, I wonder if they'll keep going south, or head west to Wyoming," Deadly said.

"Maybe Gloria can tell us," Clint said.

"Me? How would I know?"

"You've been dogging their trail," Clint said. "Make a guess. Have they left their mark on Iowa? Or Wyoming?"

"Iowa, yeah," she said. "I tracked them through Iowa. I don't think they've done anything in Wyoming, though."

"There you go," Clint said. "An educated guess—Wyoming."

"So what, we should just head for Wyoming, maybe cut 'em off?"

"We don't have to do anything that drastic yet," Clint said. "If Gloria is right—and she seems to have been up to now—they'll leave us a trail."

"But in the event we need to make a guess," Deadly said, "we've got one."

"Yes, we do," Clint said.

After breakfast they all did their assigned jobs and came together in front of the general store. Deadly and Clint had rationed out the supplies into five burlap sacks, and they tied one of them to each of their saddles.

Clint caught Deadly looking off, up and down the street.

"You thinking that lawman's going to change his mind?" Clint asked.

"I just can't believe he'd do nothin'," Deadly said. "I mean, I know what you said about evidence is true, but still . . ."

"Forget it, Walter," Clint said. "Just accept that you're more lawman than he'll ever be."

THIRTY-THREE

Nutty Pettigrew took the frying pan off the fire, walked around, and scraped some bacon and beans onto the plates of his cousins and brother, and then his own.

"Bacon and beans for breakfast?" Lyle complained.

"All we got, cuz."

"Jesus," Lyle said, "we'll have to get supplies the next place we come to."

Nutty knew that Lyle didn't care if they came to a house, a town, or a church, he was going to get some supplies.

He picked up the coffeepot and gave everybody some coffee.

"Last of it," he said.

"Christ," Lyle said, "if you guys were less interested in rape we could be gettin' ourselves more supplies before we burn a place down."

"What's more interestin' than rape?" Joe asked.

"Nothin', far as you're concerned," Lyle said. "You know, you're a sick man, Joe."

"Yeah, yeah, you tol' me that before, but I didn't see you skippin' your turn, did I?"

"Well, I ain't stupid," Lyle said. "If it's there, I'm gonna tear me off a piece."

"Christ, you're all sick," Deacon said. "Ya didn't see me stickin' my prick into some little girl, didja?"

Joe laughed and said, "That's only 'cause you didn't want sloppy fourths, cousin."

"It's because I'd rather have sex with a woman than with some kid."

"Hey," Joe said, "a hole is a hole, am I right? Huh?"

"Not when they're too young to even get wet," Deacon said.

"Wet, dry, I still get in there," Joe said happily.

Lyle studied his brother Joe. Ten years younger than Lyle's thirty-five, Joe was getting more and more out of control when it came to females. Lyle had promised their ma on her deathbed that he'd take care of her little baby, Joe, but Lyle was starting to think that the best thing he could do for his little brother was put him down.

"Where we headin' from here, Lyle?" Joe asked. "We ain't gonna stay in Iowa, are we?"

"We're wanted in Iowa," Nutty said. "We can't stay here."

"Nutty's right," Lyle said. "We're gonna head for Wyoming."

"We ain't never been to Wyoming," Deacon said.

"What about Jerry?" Joe asked, looking at Lyle.

"Your brother's dead, Joe," Lyle said. "If he wasn't, he'd be here by now."

"Damn," Joe said. "You think some lawman got him?"

"Or some husband."

Joe chuckled. Most of what he knew about women he'd learned from Jerry.

"You're runnin' out of brothers, Lyle," Nutty said, "and we're runnin' out of cousins."

"Maybe that bitch that got Lemuel got Jerry, too," Deacon said.

"We should find her and kill her," Joe said. "But rape her first."

"If I read that bitch right, you'll get your chance, Joe," Lyle said.

"Whatayamean?"

"I mean she's gonna keep comin' until she finds us," Lyle said. "Then you can have her."

"That'll be my pleasure," Joe said. "I'll tear that bitch up."

Lyle figured sooner or later he was going to have to get himself away from his family. They were all crazy.

THIRTY-FOUR

The posse crossed into Iowa and then turned immediately west. They found a cold camp just over the border. Lastings and Clint both read the sign on the ground and decided that four men had camped, then headed west when they broke camp.

"So we're going to follow their trail now?" Deadly asked. "What if it's not them?"

"Then we'll be goin' a hell of a long way out of our way," Lastings said.

"It's got to be them," Clint said. "According to Gloria, they're wanted in Iowa. They wouldn't stay any longer than they absolutely had to."

"You're assumin' they're smart," Deadly said.

"They don't have to be smart," Clint said, "just cunning, and experienced at running. I think it's our best bet, Sheriff."

Deadly knew that Clint's calling him "Sheriff" was just a concession to the badge he wore.

"Well, I'm not gonna tell you you're wrong," Deadly said. "So we'll head west. Lastings, you go on and ride up ahead of us."

"Sure thing, Sheriff."

"Soon as you see somethin', you let us know."

"Right, Sheriff."

Lastings gigged his horse into a gallop. In moments he was out of sight.

They started riding in his wake, Clint and Deadly side by side at the front, with Gloria and Caleb side by side behind them. Ever since Cottonwood, Caleb had been acting like a lovesick puppy around Gloria. It was starting to get on her nerves.

"Do you want some water, Gloria?" he asked.

"No."

"How about some peppermint candy? I bought some back in town."

"No."

"I got some beef jerky—"

"No!" she said. "Caleb, could you just shut up for a while?"

"Sure, Gloria," Caleb said. "I can shut up. Don't you worry."

Up ahead Clint smiled at what he was hearing behind him, but sobered when he looked over at Walter Deadly. The longer they were out, the more and more intense the man was getting. It was plain that he had more aptitude as an undertaker than he had as a lawman, but he was still intent on doing the job. Clint only hoped that what happened when they caught up to the Pettigrews didn't change Walter Deadly for the worst—and change him irrevocably.

Sheriff Walter Deadly was wishing he had never left Bedford. In fact, he wished he had never left his place of business.

Damn it, he was an undertaker, he wasn't a lawman. He wasn't a gunman. And he wasn't a tracker. What the hell was he doing out here in the middle of nowhere, trying to track down a gang of killers?

All along Deadly had been grateful to Clint Adams for coming with them, but now he knew that Adams was the only reason he couldn't turn back. He would lose too much face. On the other hand, if Clint had not been along, then he could have turned back when all the others did, not worrying about what anybody thought of him.

He didn't even care what the woman, Gloria, thought of him. If Clint Adams hadn't been riding right there next to him, he would have turned back.

THIRTY-FIVE

Compared to Minnesota, Wyoming was heaven, even though Clint still had to wear his jacket.

"Okay," Deadly said, looking out over the expanse of land ahead of them, "we're in Wyoming. Now what?"

"Maybe Lastings will find something for us," Clint said.

"Maybe he'll lose Caleb," Gloria said hopefully. Her horse was drinking from the small water hole they'd stopped at.

At her request, Clint had started letting the kid ride with Lastings. He told him maybe he'd learn something. Gloria appreciated the quiet time.

Deadly looked done in. Even his horse's head was drooping.

"Let's take a break," Clint suggested.

He dismounted and walked Eclipse over to the water hole.

Deadly remained mounted for a few moments, then dismounted slowly. Clint had the feeling he hadn't ridden this hard in a long time—maybe ever.

"You all right?" he asked.

"I don't really do a lot of riding as an undertaker," the man said, letting his horse drink.

"You've been doing pretty good up to now."

"Yeah, well, it only started to hurt . . . well, a while back."

"See if you can stretch it out," Clint said.

"It's not my back so much as it's my . . ."

"I get it," Clint said. "The only thing that'll fix that, believe it or not, is more riding."

"Well, that's what we're gonna be doin'," Deadly said, "for a while."

Clint knew that Deadly was starting to feel sorry he'd ever started this—probably sorry he'd ever accepted the job of sheriff. But Clint couldn't let the man know he knew that.

"I guess we better hit the saddle again," he said.

"Right," Deadly said, "but let's fill our canteens first."

"Good idea. Gloria?"

"I heard," she said. "I'm filling it now."

Clint filled his own canteen and hung it on his saddle. Gloria came over to stand next to him.

"Is he all right?" she asked.

"He's a little out of his element."

"I think we all are, except you."

"Yeah," Clint said, "I've noticed that."

"Why don't you tell him to forget it and go back home?" she said. "He can take Lastings and the kid with him. And then you can go your way."

"And you'll go yours?"

"That's right."

"Which is after the Pettigrews."

"Right again."

"Alone?"

"That's what I've been doing for a while," she said, "taking care of myself."

"Well," Clint said, "he may be out of his element, but I don't think he'd go for that."

"You could stay with me," she suggested. "We can

probably move faster without them. And we don't need to have his badge with us when we catch up to them."

"So you can just kill them?"

"Exactly."

"I don't think that's going to work, Gloria," Clint said, "but if you want to approach him with the idea, be my guest."

She turned and looked over at Deadly, who was filling his canteen . . . slowly.

"No," she said, "I'd probably just embarrass him."

"Good point."

"And by the time we do catch up to them," Clint said, "he may be ready to forget he's wearing a badge. Besides, it doesn't really mean very much in Wyoming."

"You're probably right. Hey, I've got somethin' to ask you."

"What?"

"Back in Cold Creek, how did you know I'd be able to make that shot? The whiskey bottle."

"Back when we met, I realized you had a natural aptitude with a gun."

"Yeah, but that was a trick shot."

"I figured you'd probably been practicing since then."

"I have," she said, "but you know what? I've never been able to make that shot before."

He smiled.

"You two ready to go?" Deadly asked. He'd already mounted up.

"Yeah, we're ready," Clint said.

"Yep," Gloria said, "we are."

THIRTY-SIX

"You know," Gloria said to Clint and Deadly a while later, "there's no way we can bring them back for killing the lawmen, or the family."

"Why's that?" Deadly asked.

"Because they never leave witnesses," she said. "A judge is gonna give you the same story that sheriff back in Cottonwood did."

Clint knew what she was doing. She was trying to get Deadly to forget about taking them back to stand trial.

"You might be right."

"It would probably be easier to take care of them when we catch up, instead of trying to bring them all the way back to Minnesota."

"Take care of them?" Deadly asked. "You mean kill them?"

"If we have to."

Clint thought Deadly would protest, but the man surprised him by saying, "You might be right about that, too."

"You'd have to take off that badge and put it in your pocket," Clint said. "Not even take it out until you get back home."

Without hesitating, Deadly unpinned the star on his chest and put it in his pocket.

"I don't even think I'll take it out of my pocket when I get home, except to give it back."

"You're done?" Clint asked.

"I'm done when I get back home. This isn't for me, Clint."

Clint knew they could talk about it now, because it was Deadly himself who'd brought it up—the part about being out of his element anyway.

"Who am I kiddin'?" he asked. "I'm an undertaker, not a lawman."

"Why'd you take the job then?"

"Nobody else wanted it," he said, "and face it, that town is so small I never thought we even needed a lawman. Hell, we hardly need an undertaker."

"How'd you end up there?" Clint asked.

"You might not believe it, but the town wasn't always that small. It burned down about ten years ago—most of it anyway. Some of us are just tryin' to keep it goin'."

They were quiet for a while and then Gloria, riding with Clint between her and Deadly, said, "Why?"

"Why what?"

"Why try to keep it goin'?" she asked. "Why not just leave and let it die?"

"You know," Deadly said, "a couple of days ago I would've had an answer for you. Now I'm thinking . . . well yeah, why?"

Gloria came from a town a lot bigger than Bedford, but hers had died long ago. It took more than buildings to make a town.

"Why go back, then, Walter?" she asked.

"That might be something I have to think about," he admitted.

"Look," Clint said, pointing ahead. "Lastings and the kid."

They reined in and waited.

"Well, they didn't waste any time," Lastings said.

"What happened?" Deadly asked.

"It's bad," Caleb said.

"You better just come and see for yourselves," Lastings said.

THIRTY-SEVEN

When they came within sight of the carnage, they reined in and stared. They were on a rise, looking down into a valley.

"Is that a town?" Deadly asked.

"Was it a town?" Gloria asked.

"It looks more like . . . a compound."

"Have you been down there, Lastings?" Deadly asked.

"Yeah, we rode down."

"Any survivors?"

"None."

"No witnesses," Gloria said.

"All right," Clint said, "let's get down there and see what we can learn."

Clint looked over at Deadly, trying to send him a message, but he needn't have bothered. They were on the same page.

"Lastings, you and the kid keep ridin' ahead," Deadly said. "Clint and I will see what we can learn here."

"Okay, Boss. Come on, kid."

"What about Gloria?" Caleb asked.

Lastings put his arm around Caleb's shoulders.

"Kid, forget about that girl," he said. "She'd chew you up and spit you out."

"She's a nice girl," Caleb argued.

"You got a lot to learn about women, kid," Lastings said. He was about five years older than Caleb, but he was talking as if he was a lot older. "Mount up," he said.

As Lastings and Caleb rode off, Clint, Deadly, and Gloria surveyed the carnage.

"What happened here?" Gloria asked. "There's no sign of a fire."

"It looks like there were two houses and a barn," Clint said. "This is not a ranch, and I don't see any sign that it's a farm."

"Like you said," Deadly replied. "Looks like a compound."

"Compound?" Gloria asked.

"Two families living on the same land, but in separate houses," Clint said.

"Sharing everything else," Deadly said.

Gloria looked around, saw the bodies in the rubble.

"How many dead?" she asked.

"That's what we're going to find out," Clint said. "Do you want to leave it to Walter and me?"

"No," she said, "I'll do my part."

"Okay," Deadly said, "let's do it."

What they discovered was that the buildings had been pulled down, in some cases with the people still inside. Some of the people had died that way, while others had clearly been shot.

Each house had one family in it, husband, wife, and children—one child in one house, and two in the other. A total of seven dead. The youngest of the dead children seemed to have been a three-year-old girl. She had died when a beam fell on her.

"Goddamn them," Gloria said. "Look at the children. That poor baby . . ."

They stood there in silence, wondering what drove men

to do what the Pettigrews had done here. What would ever make them think to pull people's homes down around them? Why not just burn them down like they had the For- resters' home? Were they out of matches?

Then they heard it, only because they had all been stunned into silence.

Crying.

Gloria turned around.

"Is that . . . a child?"

"Sounds like it," Clint said.

"My God," Gloria said. "Where?"

They started moving about, trying to find where the cry- ing was coming from.

"Here!" Gloria cried out. She was standing knee-deep in the rubble of the barn.

Clint and Deadly joined her there and started digging through the debris.

"Hello! We can hear you," Gloria shouted. "We can hear you. Don't be frightened. Call out to us."

Suddenly, the cry became cries of "Help! Help!" and then Clint saw it. He uncovered a trapdoor in the floor of the barn.

He opened it and saw a girl inside—not a baby, but a child of eight or nine.

"It's okay, sweetie," Gloria said, reaching down for her, "it's okay."

Gloria and Clint pulled her out of the hole, and then Gloria wrapped the child in her arms and took her away from the carnage.

They kept the child away from the other buildings, not wanting her to see the dead bodies. Gloria gave her some water, kept hugging her and talking to her.

"What should we do?" Deadly asked.

"Let Gloria deal with it," Clint said. "She'll have to tell the child her family is dead. We might as well bury them."

"That's gonna take us a while," Deadly said. "I don't want to fall any further behind."

"We'll put them in a shallow grave, just deep enough to keep critters away. We can stop at the next town and have them send out a burial detail."

"Yeah, unless the sheriff there's got some reason not to," Deadly said.

Clint looked over to where Gloria was talking to the child.

"That child is not a baby," Clint said. "She's got to be what, eight? Nine?"

"So?"

"So don't you see what that means?"

"No, what?

"The Pettigrews may have left behind their first witness."

THIRTY-EIGHT

Clint walked over to where Gloria and the child were sitting. He and Deadly had finished digging the shallow graves and had used some of the wood from the rubble to cover them up. Then they used some more wood to mark the place.

"How is she?" Clint asked.

"Shh," Gloria said. She still had her arm around the child. "She's cried herself to sleep."

"Can't say I blame her," Clint said. "Did you tell her . . . ?"

"That her whole family is dead? Yes."

"Gloria, this is important," Clint said. "Did she see anything?"

"I don't know."

"She's the only person the Pettigrews have left behind alive," Clint said. "We may have our only witness here."

"She's just a little girl."

"All she would have to do is recognize one of them," Clint said. "You have to ask her."

"Not now."

"No," Clint said. "Not now, but when we get to the next town."

"All right," Gloria said. "I'll ask her . . . soon."

"We have to get going," Clint said. "We want to get some men from the next town to come out here and bury these people properly."

"Clint, we have to find these bastards," Gloria said with feeling.

"I know."

"We have to find them and kill them."

"I know that, too, Gloria."

"I mean it," she said. "I don't want to turn them over to the law, I want to kill them."

"I understand, Gloria," he said. "I'm not arguing with you."

"And don't let him argue with me either," she said, indicating Walter Deadly with a jerk of her chin.

"I'm pretty sure he feels the same way, Gloria," he said.

"Well, he better," she said, "because I will go through anybody to see these men dead. Do you understand? Anybody!"

Clint could hear the determination in her voice, and see it in her eyes. She was more than ready to kill every member of the gang.

Clint walked around the grounds once again, trying to find something that would help them track the gang. When he thought he'd found something, he called Deadly over.

"What is it?"

"This looks like where the gang left the horses while they . . . went on a rampage."

"I see a bunch of hoofprints, Clint. That don't mean a thing to me."

They managed to wrap the survivor in a blanket. She flinched when Clint lifted her, but relaxed when he handed her up to Gloria.

"Come closer," Clint said to Deadly.

Clint pointed to the soft ground as he explained.

"One of them is riding a smaller pony. See the difference? Front hoofs to rear? It's a smaller, lighter animal, probably the most sure-footed of all their horses, but certainly the most readable."

Deadly frowned.

"And you can see that in these tracks?"

"Yes."

"And can you track them that way?"

"Yes," Clint said, then added, "as long as they don't get rid of this pony at some time."

"Maybe we'll catch up to them before that," Deadly said hopefully.

"I think we will."

"Think, or know?"

"Right now I'm going to stick with think," Clint said, "but this much carnage took a while. Long enough for us to maybe close ground on them a bit."

Suddenly, Deadly got excited. "So how far behind them do you think we are?"

"I think we're a day behind, maybe a day and a half."

"That's pretty good, considering we left Cold Creek three days behind them."

"Well, we had an advantage right from the start," Clint pointed out.

"What's that?"

"We're not stopping to kill people."

Clint mounted up and looked over at Deadly. "She hasn't said a word yet."

"She's not gonna be much of a witness if she doesn't talk," Deadly pointed out.

"Well, she's talked with Gloria, but she won't say a thing to me. Obviously the result of watching a bunch of men kill her family."

"Maybe she'll talk by the time we get to the next town," Deadly offered.

"I guess we'll find that out when we get there, wherever 'there' is."

THIRTY-NINE

The town was called Damnation.

"You've got to be kiddin'," Sheriff Deadly said.

"What the hell," Gloria said. "It's the next town."

"That's a town called Damnation," the sheriff said, "and my name is Deadly. You think I wanna go down there?"

Suddenly, behind him, he heard Lastings and Caleb laughing.

"This ain't funny."

Clint said, "Maybe we can get by without telling anybody your real name."

"Maybe we should call him Sheriff Walter," Lastings suggested.

"Deadly," the sheriff said, "it's a good name for an undertaker."

"Yeah, it is."

"It's even a good name for a lawman."

Clint didn't respond.

"It's just not a good name to be goin' down there with."

"Sheriff—" Clint said.

Deadly took a deep breath.

"We better go down," Deadly said. "Those people need to be properly buried."

Deadly got his horse moving, Lastings and Caleb followed. Clint stayed back until Gloria came up beside him, with the girl riding in front of her, holding onto the saddle horn.

"How is she?"

"How do you think she is?"

"She looks like she's asleep."

Gloria took a peek. "She has been for a while."

"Okay," he said, "let's see if we can find some place for her to stay."

"In a town called Damnation?"

"I admit," he said, "it's not a great name for a town."

They started riding.

"You ever hear of it before?" she asked.

"No."

"Maybe it used to be called somethin' else."

"That's true," Clint said. "I knew a man who made the people paint their town red—literally—and rename it Hell."

"Why does that make me want to laugh?" she asked.

"Didn't make those townspeople laugh, that's for sure."

In Damnation they split up. Lastings, Caleb, and Gloria went to the hotel. Clint and Deadly rode to the sheriff's office.

"Sheriff Carl White. What can I do for you gents?" the sheriff asked, getting to his feet.

"We're a posse out of Cold Creek, Minnesota," Deadly said.

"You're a long way from home."

"We're hunting a gang called Pettigrew."

"All of 'em are Pettigrews?" the man asked. "The whole gang?"

"Brothers and cousins."

Sheriff White sat down. He was carrying too much belly to stand for too long. Had probably been carrying it for ten years or so, since he turned fifty. His chair protested.

"You think they're comin' here?"

"We think they've been here," Clint said.

"Why?"

"There's a family lives about twelve miles outside of town? To the east. Two homes on one plot of ground?"

"The Karch family. What about 'em?"

"They're all dead," Deadly said.

"What?" He sat forward.

"Except for a little girl," Clint said, "eight or nine years old."

"Jeez, that'll be Sally. What happened to her?"

"She hid in a root cellar beneath the barn," Clint said. "But she saw some of it."

"Jesus," White said.

"Does she have any family in town?"

"What? No, the whole family lived out on that compound. They preferred it that way. Only ever came to town for supplies. No family, and no friends, really. They were just . . . neighbors."

"Well," Deadly said, "now they're dead neighbors."

"And you think this Pettigrew gang did it?"

Deadly nodded.

"They would have needed supplies," Clint said. "They had to have stopped here."

"Well, we had some hard cases here, but they didn't cause any trouble."

"When were they here?"

"Two days ago."

Clint and Deadly exchanged a glance.

"We thought we were only a day behind them," Clint said.

"You are," Sheriff White said. "They rode out yesterday."

"Which way?"

"Don't know for sure, but I can probably find out from Ted Lilly. He owns the livery."

"If you don't mind, we'll ask him," Deadly said.

"Which one of you is runnin' the posse?" the man asked.

Deadly took the badge from his pocket, showed it, and returned it. "That'd be me."

"Sure," White said. "Tell Ted I sent you over."

"Thanks."

"I'll get a burial party out to the Karch place come mornin'."

"Thanks."

As Clint and Deadly started to walk out, the sheriff called out, "You lookin' to bring them in?"

"We're lookin' to kill them."

"Don't that make you a lynch mob, not a posse?" White asked.

Deadly turned to face the man. "I prefer to think of us as a posse with a lynch mob mentality."

"That could cost you your job, you know."

Deadly smiled. "Don't I know it."

"Hey," the sheriff called when they were almost out the door. "What's your name, Sheriff?"

"Walter Deadly."

He and Clint left.

"Sheriff Deadly?" White said aloud.

FORTY

Clint and Deadly saw that the other horses were in front of the hotel, so they took all the animals to the livery after Clint found Caleb in the lobby and told him. The kid said that Lastings and Gloria had taken the little girl to the room she would share with Gloria. Clint told the kid to keep waiting in the lobby.

At the livery they found a fiftyish-looking, portly man who said he was Ted Lilly.

"The sheriff said you could help us," Deadly said. "We're interested in four men who left town yesterday."

"Yeah, I know who you mean," Lilly said. "I don't mind tellin' you them four scared the bejesus outta me."

"How so?" Clint asked.

"They was saddlin' their horses to leave and one of them says to the other one, 'I didn't get to rape a woman here. Why do we gotta go?'

"The other one—older, I think he was his brother—says, 'Shut up, Joe. We're leavin'. You can have all the women you want when we get to Ludlow.'"

"Ludlow?" Deadly said. "They said they was goin' to Ludlow?"

"I guess," Lilly answered. "I don't know if they was

goin' straight there, but Ludlow's pretty famous around these parts."

"Famous for what?" Clint asked.

"Whorehouses," Lilly said. "Supposed to have more whorehouses than any other three towns around here."

"How far is Ludlow from here?" Deadly asked excitedly.

"Sixty miles, due west," Lilly said. "You can't miss it. Them crazy women put out signs leadin' you to town. You started seein' 'em while you're still twenty miles away."

"Ludlow," Deadly said, looking at Clint. "Sixty miles. We can make that tonight."

"In the dark?" Clint asked. "That's a good way to lose a good horse. I say we leave in the morning."

"What if they leave Ludlow in the mornin' as we're leavin' here?"

"Jesus, Walter," Clint said, "they could've skipped Ludlow, or they could be there now dippin' their wicks. Or they could've made another raid between here and there. We don't know what they're doing, but that doesn't mean we should risk our horses—and our necks—by riding at night. Morning's good enough."

"Okay, if you say so."

"You leavin' your horses or not?" Lilly asked.

"Leaving them," Clint said. He slapped Eclipse's neck. "Make sure you take good care of this one."

"Mister," Ted Lilly said, "I know a good horse when I see one."

"We'll want them at first light," Clint said.

"At first light I'll be havin' breakfast," Lilly said. "That is, unless you want to pay extree for my time."

"We'll pay," Clint said.

"Then I'll be here, and your animals will be ready."

"Thanks."

"When we tell Gloria, she's gonna wanna head right out," Deadly said.

"She'll listen to me," Clint said, "but I think Lastings and the kid should stay behind."

"Why?"

"They're liable to get killed when we catch up to the gang," Clint said, "or get us killed."

"What about Gloria?"

"The woman can shoot," Clint said. "That's more than I know about Lastings and Caleb's abilities with a gun. I say we leave them here."

"Well . . . I guess that's okay," Deadly said. "Three against four, and I got the Gunsmith as one of my three. Sounds even."

"Even?" Clint said. "Let's hope not."

They headed for the door, but Clint stopped short.

"Hey, Mr. Lilly?"

"Yeah?"

"Is there any law in Ludlow?"

"Is there?" Lilly said. "Sheriff's Nelson Quinn. Nels owns two of the whorehouses himself."

FORTY-ONE

Clint knocked on the door of the room Gloria was sharing with the little girl.

"Oh, hello, Clint," Gloria said, cracking the door. "She's asleep."

"Step out into the hall then," Clint said.

She did, and closed the door behind her, leaving it cracked a bit so she could hear.

"Did you get her name yet?"

"First name. Sally."

"Her last name's Karch. The sheriff's going to send out a burial party in the morning."

"That's good. Does she have any family in town?" Gloria asked.

"No."

"Maybe a friend that can take Sally?"

"No friends. They kept to themselves."

"What's gonna happen to the girl?"

"I don't know, Gloria. Look, we have to leave in the morning."

"To go where?"

"A town called Ludlow."

"Is that where they are?"

"It's our best bet," he said. "The sheriff and I have decided to leave Lastings and Caleb behind. We don't know how they'll react in a firefight. I don't want to get killed looking out for them."

"So just you, me, and the sheriff?"

"Yes," he said, "and just between you and me, I'm not so sure about him either."

"You and me then."

He nodded, and said, "Unless you want to stay behind with the girl."

"No," she said, "I'm goin'."

"Caleb and Lastings can look out for her until we get back."

"Are we comin' back here?"

"Well, I thought you'd want to, to see to it that someone takes the girl in."

"Well, yeah, I could do that."

"Okay, well, I'm going to get something to eat and then turn in."

"Can you bring somethin' for me and Sally? We can eat in the room."

"I'll take care of it."

"Gloria," the child's voice called from the room. There was a touch of panic in her tone.

"She's awake. I gotta go."

Gloria went back inside, and Clint went back down to the lobby. Caleb was still there.

"Where's Lastings?"

"I dunno, Clint," Caleb said.

"Well, come on, kid, let's go get something to eat. I want to talk to you."

Deadly had gone to his room for a while. He said he'd eat on his own.

"Hey, great. I'm starving."

"So am I."

"What about Gloria?"

"We'll bring something back for her and the girl."

"Whatja wanna talk to me about?" Caleb asked as they went out the door.

"Let's wait until we're sitting down in a restaurant."

He put his arm around the kid.

Over steaks Clint told Caleb that he and Deadly and Gloria would be going to Ludlow in the morning, but that Caleb would not be going with them.

"Why not?"

"Let me put it to you this way," Clint said. "I don't want you to get killed, and I don't want to get killed watching out for you."

"I can shoot," the boy said.

"Maybe you can," Clint said, "but I don't have the time to find out."

"What about Lastings?" he asked.

"He's staying behind, too."

"But Gloria's going?"

"Yes."

"She'll think I'm a coward."

"Not at all," Clint said. "In fact, Caleb, she probably won't think about you at all."

"What?"

"She's got a lot of other things on her mind, Caleb," Clint said. "You have to forget about her."

"Oh, I get it," Caleb said. "She's your girl, right?"

"She's nobody's girl, kid," Clint said. "Believe me, she doesn't have time for that."

"Will you be comin' back here?"

"Yes," Clint said. "Gloria's going to want to check on Sally."

"Sally?"

"The little girl."

"Oh."

"In fact," Clint said, "If you really want to do something

for Gloria, you'll make sure Sally is safe while we're gone."

"Babysit, you mean?" Caleb was appalled.

"Don't think of it that way," Clint said. "Come on, eat up. Whatever you end up doing tomorrow, we're going to have to get an early start."

When Clint and Caleb got back to the hotel, he sent the boy to his room. He got Lastings's room number from the clerk, but when he knocked there was no answer. He was going to have to tell him in the morning that he wasn't going to Ludlow, land of the whorehouses.

Clint thought about knocking on Deadly's door, but then remembered he was supposed to bring Gloria and Sally some food. So he left the hotel again. He'd drop off their food and then retire to his own room and bed. With any luck this would all end tomorrow.

FORTY-TWO

Deadly knocked on Clint's door before first light.

"Let's get this over with," he suggested.

"Lilly might not be at the livery."

"So what? We'll wake him up."

"I never got a chance to talk to Lastings to tell him he's not coming."

"Did you talk to the kid?"

"Yes, him I got to."

"Let him tell Lastings. Come on, I'll go to the livery and you get Gloria."

"She'll have to get Caleb to watch Sally."

"Who's Sally?"

"The little girl."

"Oh, yeah," Deadly said. "Okay, well, let's get movin'."

"All right," Clint said, "I'm with you."

Since Clint was already dressed, he only had to strap on his gun, fetch his rifle and saddlebags, and walk down the hall to Gloria's room.

When Clint and Gloria got to the livery, Deadly had their horses saddled.

"Ready to go?" Deadly asked Gloria.

"I'm ready."

He handed her the reins of her horse and mounted his own.

Clint took Eclipse's reins and mounted him. Deadly took off at a trot and Gloria followed. Clint knew that once they cleared town, they'd have to move fast. They wanted to cover the whole sixty miles as quickly as they could.

At some point, since he had the superior horse, he figured to ride on ahead and get to Ludlow well ahead of Deadly and Gloria.

And he had plans.

In Ludlow, Lyle Pettigrew made sure he did not go to the same whorehouse as his brother and his cousins. For one thing, Joe was likely to raise hell there, and he didn't want to hear it. Also, he didn't want his cousins and brother to know where to find him when they got themselves into trouble.

In fact, he so didn't want them to be able to find him that he decided to spend the night at the whorehouse and not his hotel room.

He woke to the snoring of the whore whose bed he was sharing. She was a pale, big-busted blonde in her thirties, which was basically why he had picked her. A lot of the others were younger—some still in their teens. He wanted to be with a woman, not a girl.

However, he didn't like snoring women.

She was lying on her belly, her bare butt visible because she had kicked off the bedclothes.

"Stop snorin', damn it!" he snapped, and slapped her ass soundly, leaving a red handprint behind.

She screamed and came awake, but she didn't react physically. She turned her head to look at him.

"Honey," she said, "you ain't one of them that likes to do it in the mornin', are ya?"

"I ain't as a rule, but if you turn over, you could convince me."

"Well, I ain't gonna turn over." He'd already paid her, so she had no qualms about sending him off without a morning poke.

Of course, Lyle being a Pettigrew, he had other ideas . . .

Late in the afternoon Lyle walked into the Cloverdale Saloon and found his brother and cousins sitting there among the other patrons. He sat down with them.

"Joe, get me a beer, will ya?" he asked.

"Sure, Lyle."

"Sleepin' late, Lyle?" Deacon asked.

"Actually, I woke up early, but I been busy since then," he said. "Seems my whore didn't figure I was paid up till mornin'."

"Whatja do to her, Lyle?" Joe asked, hurrying back with the beer so he wouldn't miss any of the story.

"Well, Joe," he said, using the glass to make wet circles on the table, "I guess I found out that I'm as crazy as any of you are."

"You done for her, Lyle?" Joe asked, gleefully. "You done for the whore?"

"Let's just say she won't be makin' any money for a while," Lyle said, drinking from his mug.

"I busted mine up some," Joe said, "but I didn't kill 'er."

"We gonna have ta leave town, Lyle?" Nutty asked.

Lyle looked across the table at his cousin, then said, "You, Nutty. I thought it was a toss-up between you and Joe who was the craziest, but it ain't. Turns out none of you is crazier than me."

"We're all crazy, Lyle," Joe said, grabbing his beer. "That's what makes this family fun."

"We gonna wait for the sheriff, Lyle?" Deacon asked. "He's bound to come after what we did to our whores. This town really likes its whores."

"And the sheriff owns a couple of the houses," Joe pointed out.

"Yeah, we'll wait," Lyle said. "I been tryin' to keep you boys under control all these months, but today I lost control, so we're all in the same boat, ain't we? So we'll wait for the sheriff, and after we take care of him, we'll pick this town clean."

"And burn it to the ground?"

"And burn it to the ground."

Sheriff Nelson Quinn knew he had to do something. He couldn't afford to let someone tear up a couple of his girls, and some from another house, and let them get away with it.

He didn't have a deputy. Ludlow wasn't a big town, but there was never much law keeping to do. It had a specialty, and men came for that. They weren't usually looking for trouble.

This bunch was different. This bunch he'd have to send packing.

He grabbed a rifle from his gun rack and headed for the saloon.

When the sheriff entered, Joe saw him and nudged Lyle underneath the table.

"He's here," Joe said.

"You boys know what to do," Lyle said. "You crazy sons of bitches."

The sheriff looked around, spotted them at their table, and started over. He'd hardly gotten his mouth open, or his hands unhooked from his belt, when all four Pettigrews rose, drew, and fired. They kept firing into his body long after he was on the floor, dead. By the time they stopped firing, the saloon had emptied out.

"Now what?" Joe asked Lyle.

"Now we pick it clean."

FORTY-THREE

Clint got to Ludlow late in the afternoon. Deadly and Gloria would be along in half an hour, maybe an hour. At first they'd tried to match Eclipse's pace, but in the end they had fallen back. They probably also had to stop to rest their mounts.

Clint rode into Ludlow and stopped at the sheriff's office. No one was there. He left, and had stopped just outside to figure his next move when he heard the shots.

Lyle watched from the street as his brother and cousins looted the town. They started by raiding the whorehouses, taking all the money they were holding. The first one, owned by the sheriff, tried to resist, until the madam was told that Sheriff Nelson Quinn was dead.

The piano player was shot and killed in another house.

As Lyle watched Joe, Deacon, and Nutty enter the last of the whorehouses, he saw some of the girls come out onto the second-floor balcony. He drew his gun and fired up at them, driving them back inside.

"Back inside," he shouted, "like the rest of the scared rabbits in this town!"

It was true. Once the Pettigrews had started shooting and looting, the streets were abandoned. The people were all inside with their doors locked, waiting to see if they were going to be next.

Clint walked toward the sound of the shots, and stopped in front of a store where a man and woman were staring out the window. He knocked on the door and the man cracked it a bit to talk to him.

"What's going on?" he asked.

"Bunch of fellers are shootin' up the town, lootin' the whorehouses. We got to stay inside to protect our property." The man was holding a rifle, but he didn't seem very comfortable with it.

"This town got a telegraph key?" Clint asked.

"No."

"How about a bank?"

"Oh yeah, we got a bank."

"Only one?"

"Just one."

"Okay then," Clint said. "Stay inside."

"Mister?"

"Yeah?"

"They killed the sheriff earlier today," the man said. "Shot him down like a dog. He never had a chance."

"Okay, thanks," Clint said. "Inside."

Clint had two ideas. One, just go to the bank and wait. The second idea was to sneak a peek at whatever the Pettigrews were doing at the moment, and pick his spot. Maybe he could isolate them and take them one at a time.

He heard another shot and decided to see what was going on.

Deacon and Nutty came out of the whorehouse with their hands full.

"Where's Joe?" Lyle demanded, although he thought he knew.

"Spotted a little gal in there he liked," Nutty said. "He took her to her room for a little fun."

"Damn it."

"Want me to go get 'im?" Nutty asked.

"Naw," Lyle said, "he'll be ass-kickin' crazy by now. He might take a shot at you. We'll let him finish and meet him at the bank."

"The bank!" Nutty said, his eyes shining.

"Put that stuff in your saddlebags and let's get movin'," Lyle said. They had their horses with them so when they were finished with the town they could ride out without delay.

Clint had secreted himself across the street and listened to the conversation. He knew that one Pettigrew was still in the house. That would work for him.

He waited until the three men left the area, then ran across the street and into the house. Immediately, he could hear a girl screaming from upstairs.

A woman who had to be the madam turned on him and glared. She had a black eye that was swollen half-shut.

"What did you forget?" she demanded. "You wanna hit me in my other eye?"

"I'm not with the gang, ma'am, I'm here to help."

The woman didn't waste any time.

"Well then, help her," she said, "before he kills her."

"What room?"

"Four!" she shouted as he started up the stairs.

He ran down the hall to room four, drew his gun, and then entered. He slammed the door open. A man was on the bed, naked, and Clint could see the kicking legs of a girl beneath him.

The man heard the door slam open and turned to look over his shoulder.

"Who are you?"

"The man who's going to stop you, Pettigrew. Which one are you?"

"Mister," Joe said, annoyed, "get out of here." He turned his attention to the girl.

The man was naked, so there was nothing else for Clint to grab but the hair on his head. Luckily, it was pretty shaggy.

He grabbed a handful and pulled with all his might. Off balance, the big man tumbled to the floor. The girl on the bed began taking big gulps of air, as if Pettigrew had been choking her.

"Don't worry," he said to her. "Get out of here."

He didn't have to tell her twice. She grabbed her clothes and ran into the hall.

"Who the hell are you?" the man on the floor asked.

"Which one are you?" Clint asked again, pointing his gun at him.

"Which what?"

"Pettigrew."

"Oh, I'm Joe."

Joe stole a glance at his gun, hanging on the bedpost.

"Go ahead, try for it," Clint invited.

"You're making a mistake, you know," Joe said. "My brother and cousins will be lookin' for me."

"That's fine," Clint said. "I'll be ready for them."

"They'll kill you."

A look at the gun again.

"You keep looking at it," Clint said. "Go ahead."

"I ain't stupid. Who are you, anyway?"

"My name's Clint Adams. I'm part of the posse that's been tracking you from Cold Creek."

"Cold Creek? We killed that sheriff."

"Yeah, well, the sheriff from Bedford put a posse together."

"So where are they?"

"I got here first," Clint said. "They'll be along."

"Wait a minute," Joe said. "Did you say . . . Clint Adams?"

"That's what I said."

"The Gunsmith?"

Clint nodded.

Suddenly, Joe Pettigrew did not seem so interested in his gun.

FORTY-FOUR

"What are we supposed to do with him?" the madam asked Clint.

"Nothing," he said. "He's tied up, and here's his gun." He handed her the gun belt.

"What about the rest of them?"

"I'm taking care of that."

"Alone?"

"There's help on the way," he promised. "Just stay inside and keep your girls inside as well."

Abruptly, one of the girls threw her arms around him. It was the girl he'd rescued from Joe Pettigrew.

"Thank you so much!"

"You're welcome."

"When you're finished, you come back," she said. "I'm gonna give you a free poke."

"Thanks," he said, extricating himself from her hold. "I'll keep that in mind."

As he started for the door, the madam grabbed his arm and said, "Good luck."

"Thanks."

* * *

As Clint left the whorehouse, he saw Gloria and Deadly riding down the street. He ran at them, waving his hands.

"Get your horses off the street," he hissed. "They're hitting the bank."

"All of 'em?" Deadly asked.

"Three of them," Clint said. "I've got one tied up in that building."

"Which one?" Gloria asked.

"What?"

"Which one of them do you have tied up?" She seemed very calm.

"Joe," Clint said. "His name is Joe."

"Where's the bank?" Deadly said.

"This way," Clint said. "Follow me. Don't fire until I do. Understood?"

Deadly nodded, and Gloria said, "Yes."

"This way," he said again.

When Lyle, Deacon, and Nutty reached the bank, the door was locked and the window shade was down.

"Nobody's here!" Nutty said, disappointed.

"They know what's happening in town," Lyle said. "They locked the door. Kick it in."

Nutty lifted his leg and kicked the door. It not only opened, it splintered. They drew their guns and rushed in.

Clint, Deadly, and Gloria came within sight of the bank just as the three Pettigrews rushed in.

"Should we wait for them to come out?" Deadly asked.

"No," Clint said, "somebody might get killed. We have to let them know we're out here."

"Won't they take a hostage?" Deadly asked.

"Not these guys," Clint said. "I don't think they're smart enough. I think they'll come out of there and shoot it out."

"Should we cover the back?" Deadly asked.

Clint almost said no, but then he looked at Gloria, and said, "Why don't you cover the back, Gloria?"

"Okay," she said. She ran across the street and down an alley that would take her to the back of the bank.

"Now what?" Deadly asked.

"Let's go announce ourselves."

They started and then stopped when Clint put his hand on Deadly's arm.

"You better put your badge on, Walter," he said. "We're going to want them to see it."

Inside, Nutty kept his gun on the three bank employees—the manager and two tellers—while Deacon and Lyle emptied the drawers and the safe.

"Look at all this money!" Deacon said

"Admire it later," Lyle said. "Just load it up."

"Pettigrew!"

They all stopped. The voice had come from outside.

"Who's that?" Nutty asked.

"I don't know," Lyle said. He looked at Deacon. "Keep working."

"Pettigrew! Inside the bank. Can you hear me?"

Lyle went to the front door and looked out. There were two men standing in the street. One of them had a badge on.

"Whataya see, Lyle?"

"Two men. One's a lawman."

"Is that all?" Nutty asked. "I thought there'd be a posse."

"Come on, Pettigrew!" the man wearing the badge shouted.

"Whataya want?" Lyle called.

"We want you to come out with your hands up."

"That ain't gonna happen."

"Then come out shootin'," the man called. "It's your choice."

"Can I think about it?" Lyle asked.

"Why not?"

"Fifteen minutes."

Lyle backed away from the door.

"What are we gonna think about, Lyle?" Nutty asked. "We ain't givin' up."

"We ain't gonna wait fifteen minutes either. Deke! Get out here!"

Deacon came out from behind a teller's cage, carrying two sacks of money.

"Put those down. We'll come back in for 'em. Nutty, you go through the window, Deke and me are going out the doors. And we go with guns a-blazin', understand?"

"Oh yeah," Nutty said. "Should I kill them?" He indicated the bank employees.

"No, they ain't gonna do nothin'," Lyle said. "Forget 'em. Get ready."

Nutty moved over to the window. Lyle and Deacon positioned themselves in front of the doors.

"Watch the windows," Clint told Deadly.

"Why? They got fifteen minutes."

"They're not going to take fifteen minutes. They'll either come through the window or throw something through. And they'll come now. You watch the windows."

Deadly drew his gun as Nutty Pettigrew came flying out the window, just like Clint had predicted.

As Nutty Pettigrew landed on his feet, roaring as loud as he could, Deadly shot him. The impact of the bullet did nothing to slow the huge man down.

Clint drew as two of the Pettigrews came through the door, guns loud. He took his time, shot one of them and put him down, then turned to the other one. But peripherally he was watching Walter Deadly.

"Again!" Clint shouted. "Shoot him again!"

Deadly fired again just as Nutty Pettigrew fired at him. His bullet hit the big man in the chest, while something dug into his right thigh. He went down to a knee and fired at Nutty again. The third bullet did the job.

Lyle rolled to the ground as he saw his brother Deacon go down. When he came up with his gun extended, Clint was ready. He fired and hit the man in the middle of his torso. The bullet just missed his heart, but as Lyle went down onto his back, he knew that he'd been killed.

It got quiet.

Clint stepped over to Deadly, helped him to his feet.

"You okay?" he asked.

"I don't know," Deadly said, his voice tight with pain, "I've never been shot before."

"Just wait here. We'll get you a doctor."

Clint walked to the big man, Nutty, who was dead. Then he checked Deacon. Dead. When he walked over to Lyle, the older Pettigrew was trying to reach his gun. Clint kicked it away. Lyle looked up at him.

"Who're you?"

"Clint Adams."

"Y-you killed me."

"I meant to," Clint said, but the man was gone.

Townspeople came running out, and two men grabbed Deadly and carried him to the doctor's office. Clint figured he'd be okay to ride back to Damnation. That would be where they'd split up. Deadly would head back to Minnesota and his undertaker's job. Today was the last day he'd wear the sheriff's badge.

Clint looked around as people came out into the street, moving toward the bank, pausing over the fallen outlaws. He didn't see Gloria anywhere. But he had an idea where she'd gone . . .

Gloria entered the whorehouse. All the girls were collected in the front hall, and the madam asked, "Is it over?"

"Almost," Gloria said. "What room?"

"Four."

She went up the stairs, along to room four, and opened the door. Joe Pettigrew looked up from the floor, where he was hogtied.

"Who the hell are you?"

"You remember Jasper, Kansas?"

"That ghost town?"

"I killed your brother Lemuel."

"You? You're that bitch—"

"And now I'm gonna kill you." She pointed her gun at him.

Joe laughed.

"You ain't got the guts to kill a man who's tied up—"

She quieted him by putting a bullet in his head. She didn't bother to untie him. She didn't care if people knew what she'd done.

She went back downstairs, looked at the madam, and said, "Now it's over."

Outside, she found Clint waiting.

"That it?" he asked.

"That's it."

"What are you going to do now?" he asked.

"I'm goin' back to Damnation. If Sally has no family, I might stay there awhile."

A long while, he thought. They headed for the doctor's office.

"I thought you were going to cover the back of the bank," he said.

She grinned and said, "No, you didn't."

He smiled and said, "You're right. I didn't."

Watch for

THE MAN WITH THE IRON BADGE

331st novel in the exciting GUNSMITH series
from Jove

Coming in July!

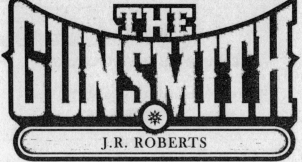

GIANT ACTION! GIANT ADVENTURE!

THE GUNSMITH

J.R. ROBERTS

penguin.com/actionwesterns

M228AS0808

GIANT-SIZED ADVENTURE FROM
AVENGING ANGEL LONGARM.

BY TABOR EVANS

2006 Giant Edition:
LONGARM AND THE
OUTLAW EMPRESS

2007 Giant Edition:
LONGARM AND THE
GOLDEN EAGLE SHOOT-OUT

2008 Giant Edition:
LONGARM AND THE
VALLEY OF SKULLS

penguin.com/actionwesterns